A NEXT GENERATION NOVELLA

# BEFORE Us

## J.M. WALKER

IBSN: 978-1-989782-11-8

Before Us (Next Generation, #3)

# FAMILY TREE

**Angel and Genevieve "Jay" Rodriguez**
(Grit, King's Harlots #1/Grim, King's Harlots #3)
Angelica "Gigi"
Ryder
Meadow

**Asher and Meeka Donovan**
(Stain, King's Harlots #2)
Aiden
Ashton

**Coby and Brogan Porter**
(Rude, King's Harlots #4/For You, King's Harlots #7)
Zachary "Zach"

**Dale and Maxine "Max" Michaels**
(Numb, King's Harlots #5)
Piper

**Vincent "Stone" and Creena Stone**
(Rust, King's Harlots #6)
Luna
Vincent Junior

**Greyson and Eve Mercer**
(Greyson, Hell's Harlem #1)
Jaron

**Tray and Zillah Lister**
(Tray, Hell's Harlem #2)
Beatrix "Bee"

**John and Beatrix "Trixie" Butcher**
(Hell's Harlem Series)
Cyrus
Samson "Sammy"

# PROLOGUE

*Piper*

**WHEN I LEFT** his bed, I wondered where I'd gone wrong. Why life was throwing these curveballs at me. At us. Why had it decided to play these evil tricks on my heart?

I was happy. Content.

And then *he* showed up.

I was in another country and he still found me. Was he looking for me? Did he even know I existed before he sat down across from me at the little café in Paris?

"Piper."

My name on his tongue was like a kiss to the back of my neck. The deep timbre slid over my body, touching every inch of me. Inside and out.

"You know who I am," I said, allowing my eyes to rake over his large form. The leather cut he was wearing did nothing to hide the muscles beneath it.

I remembered him from when I was a girl, but now I was looking at him with the eyes of a woman.

"Of course I know who you are." He sat forward, his smoky-gray eyes dropping to the cleavage poking out from my shirt. "Are you on vacation?"

"Backpacking." I noticed his full lips, my mouth watering at what it would be like to kiss him.

It had been years since I had seen Jaron Mercer. Probably since before I even hit puberty. But the way he was looking at me now made me realize that I was no longer the little girl he used to tease with the other boys we grew up with.

"Your parents let you come here by yourself?" He raised an eyebrow and licked along his full bottom lip.

Heat rushed through me, my heart picking up speed at the small movement. "Who says I'm alone?"

He smirked, causing dimples to form in his cheeks.

Letting out a slow breath, I reached for my glass of water with a shaky hand. "Are *you* on vacation?" I asked, taking a sip of the cold liquid.

His smirk grew. "I was here on business, but now I think I'll add some pleasure to this trip."

"What kind of pleasure?" I asked, suddenly curious about the man I no longer knew.

As soon as that question left my mouth, the rest of the night ended up in a blur.

Every part of me tingled with the memory of him touching me. Kissing me. *Consuming* me.

I looked back at the man lying in the bed. The white sheets hung low on his hips, the large tattoo of a skull with horns moving slightly on his back with each breath he took.

My hands tingled, itching to reach out to him and crawl back into his warmth. But I couldn't. As much as I didn't want to, I had to get home. I had to get away from the man who would destroy everything I knew and save me just the same.

# ONE

*Piper*

**IT ALL STARTED** with a look.

A touch here. A wink there. A smirk. And then dimples. Those damn dimples. They got to me every time. And the way he looked at me; like I was the only one who existed in his world even though I knew it wasn't true. It couldn't be. Our relationship, if you could call it that, was toxic. It wasn't real. It was never real. It was just a fantasy that I made up in my head. We could never be together. Although, the sex was very real. The feelings I had for him, however, were not. I refused to feel anything for the man who came to me in my dreams.

When I slipped out of the hotel room almost five weeks ago in Paris, I never expected to run into *him* again. Even though we grew up together as kids, I hadn't seen Jaron Mercer in years. Not until he showed up out of nowhere when I was backpacking through Europe and happened to make a stop in Paris. It was a small world when he sat down in front of me at the little café I'd come across. We talked for half an hour before we crashed into his hotel room and he bent me over the nearest surface.

*"You're going to remember me for the rest of your life."*

And I would. My body clenched, aching to be filled by him again even though I knew he was dangerous for me.

Jaron was more than your typical bad boy. Besides being a member of his father's motorcycle club, you wouldn't know just how *bad* he actually was until it was too late. With those silver-gray eyes of his and those damn dimples, I didn't know just how lethal he could be until he had me screaming his name and begging for more.

*"Ride my dick, Piper. Give it to me good and hard. I want my cock to motherfucking ache because of you."*

The things he had said to me. Promises. Fantasies. It was dirty talk to the extreme. I had been with other guys, but no one ever came close to him.

And now, sitting in the bar with a couple of my girlfriends, his eyes drilled into me from the other side of the large room. The tiny hairs on my body stood on end. My cheeks burned. I squirmed and shifted in my seat. All because of *him*.

"Is that …" Angelica Rodriguez smacked my arm, her caramel eyes widening. "Holy shit, girl. It is. That's Jaron Mercer. Didn't you have a crush on him at some point?"

My cheeks burned even more. I still did.

"I think we all did. Jaron Mercer." Meadow sighed, fanning herself. "He's looking so damn good these days."

I laughed, shaking my head at the two sisters who were only a few years apart but were the complete opposite in everything they did.

"Come on, Piper." Meadow pointed at me, pursing her full red lips. "You know it's true. Although, he's a little too young for me." She winked. Sitting back, she pulled her shoulder- length, black, curly hair up into a messy bun. A few curls fell, framing her face.

"Young?" Gigi frowned. "He's our age."

"Exactly." Meadow tapped her nose, a slow grin spreading on her face. "He *is* hot, but he doesn't do it for me." She met my gaze. "So, Piper. He's all yours."

I coughed, my neck heating, and took a sip of my beer. "I have no idea what you're talking about."

Gigi laughed that time. "Right, and I don't have a thing for Luna's younger brother."

"So taboo." Meadow clapped her hands together. "I love it."

Vincent Junior was the youngest out of our group of friends, but not by much. Although it made Gigi several years older than him, none of us cared. She did, so she never acted on her feelings.

"I wonder if they like pastries." Meadow took a long swig of her beer. "That's a deal-breaker, you know? They have to like sweets or they're not getting into my sweetness."

I rolled my eyes. "Oh, God."

Gigi only giggled.

While Meadow baked, Angelica, or Gigi as she liked to be called, danced. She was tall, lean, and strong. The moves I had seen her do were motivating. Although I could never dance like her, it did give me that push I needed to work out.

She was damn good at what she did, too. They both were. I, on the other hand, was stuck. I had no hobbies. Although I enjoyed drawing and painting like my mother, Maxine, did, it was just for fun. And most of my artwork was just doodling. I still hadn't found my niche, but I did enjoy traveling. Maybe I could find a job where I got paid to see the world. I bit my inner cheek to keep from sighing. Again. I had been doing that a lot lately.

"We should go say hi," Gigi suggested, taking a sip of her beer.

"How about we not." I really didn't want to talk to Jaron. No. I wanted to fuck him and have him do all the talking instead.

*"I'm going to stretch this pussy wide with my thick cock."*

I shivered, scrubbing a hand down my face as the memories of that night so many weeks ago slid into my mind.

"You okay, Piper?" Meadow asked, raising a dark brown eyebrow. "Are you fantasizing about having Jaron between those legs of yours?"

"Oh, God." I laughed. "Stop. No wonder you're still single."

"Shut up." She threw a napkin at me. "I'm single because I'm picky and no one can handle all of this." She made a motion of running her hands down her body.

"Well at least we know her ego isn't small." Gigi threw a toothpick at her sister.

"Seriously though." Meadow sighed. "I just wish a guy wouldn't be so damn skeevy when I ask him to invite a friend along. There is nothing wrong with threesomes." She pouted.

"Uh …" I took a sip of my beer. "No, there isn't."

"Yeah." Gigi turned to me, waggling her eyebrows. "How are those twins doing?"

"They want nothing to do with me since I broke it off." I shrugged. "No big deal. It's for the better."

"I'm sorry." Gigi patted my hand.

Meadow scrunched her nose. "Their loss, babe. I love those guys like brothers, but they need to move on. Especially if that's what you want."

I wasn't even sure what I wanted anymore.

"Not to make this conversation even heavier but have you girls heard from Luna?" Gigi asked, checking her phone.

"No." Meadow checked hers.

I shook my head.

Our friend had gotten into a fight with her dad over her boyfriend. It was a mess and now here we were at the bar. Drinking. While Luna went home to her boyfriend's place and was probably having wild crazy monkey sex. I was so damn jealous of her.

My center throbbed. God, even my body missed Jaron. "I'm sure she's fine." I pulled back the rest of my beer, wishing I had more all of a sudden.

"I wonder what that life is like." Gigi tapped her chin.

"What do you mean?" I stood, stretching my arms up and over my head.

"The biker life. I know our moms lived it, but it must be different for guys." Gigi shrugged. "I think I'm drunk."

I laughed. "Well then, that calls for another round." I headed to the bar and grabbed three more beers.

The hairs on the back of my neck tingled but I refused to look his way. If he wanted to talk, he could come to me. When the bartender placed the drinks on a tray, I smiled up at him and carried it over to the girls. "More beer, ladies."

"You're the best." Gigi grabbed a glass and took a large gulp. She coughed.

"Lightweight." Meadow giggled, taking her own beer.

"I think that's what our moms were trying to change," I added. All of our mothers were part of the King's Harlots motorcycle club. They were the only female MC in this area and now they volunteered at a center, known as The Dove Project, that helped human trafficking victims. "I'm just glad they never expected us to follow in their footsteps. Although, I don't think our fathers would have let that happen anyway."

"Could you imagine?" Gigi winced. "I can hear the conversation now. 'Hey, Dad, I want to become a Harlot.' His response would be, 'Over my dead fucking body'," she said in her best deep voice.

We laughed.

"No kidding." Meadow stood.

"Where are you going?" Gigi asked her.

"Bathroom." Meadow rolled her eyes. "Is that allowed, Mom?"

"Fine, fine." Gigi waved a hand in front of her, almost knocking her glass out of her other hand.

"Alright, girl." I took the glass from her and placed it on the table in front of us. "Take a moment."

She smiled at me, though it looked more like a sneer. "I love you."

"I love you too." I laughed lightly. "I think we need some water."

Three glasses of water suddenly appeared on the table.

I glanced up at the bartender.

"I overheard you." He nodded toward Gigi. "Don't need her getting sick."

"She'll be fine." I rubbed her upper back. "Won't you?"

She sighed, running her hand down my cheek. "You're so pretty."

"We'll be fine," I told the bartender. "Thank you."

He nodded once.

"Alright, girlfriend." I took her glass of beer and placed it in front of me. "I think you're cut off."

A dark shadow suddenly loomed over the table.

My heart sped up. My hands became clammy. I felt him before I saw him. The scent of leather and spice washed over me, sending my emotions into overdrive.

"Ladies." A large man placed a tray of beer on the table before sitting across from us. "Mind if we join you?"

"If you're supplying the beer—" Gigi picked a bottle off the tray "—not at all."

"I like how you think." The man nodded once, and we were surrounded.

"Hey, Gigi."

God that voice. That deep velvet voice. So smooth. So damn confident.

"Hey, Jaron. It's been awhile," Gigi slurred, making small talk with the man who had been inside my head for the past several weeks.

"It has. How's your family?" Jaron pulled up a chair and sat right beside me. He was so close, I might as well have been sitting on his lap.

"Good," she answered. "How's yours doing?"

"Not too bad. Busy as always." Jaron pulled my chair closer to his.

While they continued making small talk, I couldn't help but notice the way Jaron kept his hand on the edge of my seat. Or how his thumb brushed small circles on my hip. Or how good he smelled. God, he smelled so fucking good. Leather mixed with a hint of spice. It was man. Pure, hard man.

"How's it going, Piper?"

I chewed my bottom lip, biting back a whimper at the way my name sounded on his tongue. "Good." I looked up at him then and everything seemed to fall away from around us.

His gray eyes pierced into mine. His dark beard had grown in and was fuller than when I saw him in Paris. What I wouldn't give to feel it between my legs.

My body heated. I squirmed in my seat.

He smirked, his gaze falling to my mouth. "You look good."

My heart stuttered at the compliment.

"I still taste good too," I threw back at him, low enough for only him to hear.

His grin grew. "I bet you do."

Clearing my throat, I turned back around as Meadow returned from the bathroom.

"Ooh. Hello, boys." She waggled her eyebrows and sat at the table between the man who gave us the beer, and another one who looked at her like he wanted to be her lap dog.

I laughed, shaking my head.

"Do you ladies come here often?" asked the one who gave us beer.

"Ignore him," Jaron teased, resting his arm across the back of my chair. His thumb brushed over my bare arm. I should have worn more clothes. "He doesn't get out much. Isn't that right, old man?"

"Fuck you I don't." The man crossed his arms under his broad chest. He leaned over to Meadow. "How old are you?"

"Twenty-two." She grinned. "Why?"

The man pulled her onto his lap. "Good enough for me."

She laughed. "Don't get any ideas in that old brain of yours. My daddy would kick your ass if he knew you were rubbing your dick against me."

"Your daddy doesn't scare me," he growled in her ear. He said something else, low enough for only her to hear.

Meadow coughed, caught my gaze, and gave me a wink. "You know it's rude to tell secrets in front of people." She cupped the older man's face. "Why don't you tell our friends here what you just said?"

He raised an eyebrow.

"Yeah, Sunny," Jaron said. "Tell us what you said."

"I'd really like to hear this," the guy beside him added.

Sunny cleared his throat. "I said to her—"

"No," Meadow interrupted. "Tell them what you just said. To me."

Watching the exchange between them was something else. Meadow had always been the flirty one of our group, but I never truly saw her in action. The way she had Sunny wrapped around her finger was … hot as hell.

"Don't get any ideas, Piper," Jaron muttered.

I rolled my eyes. Not like that would happen anyway. I didn't have a dominant bone in my body.

"I said," Sunny repeated, tightening his hold on Meadow's hip, "that I want to bend you over this table, hike up this sexy as fuck dress, and make you beg for your daddy to come save you."

She grinned and patted his cheek. "Good boy."

A round of laughter erupted, but not from me. No. Instead, all I could do was stare with my jaw dropped, wishing I had even an ounce of her confidence. Holy fucking hell.

"That, guys, is my sister. A class act and the queen of flirting," Gigi teased, taking a swig of the beer I was trying to get her to stop drinking. She swayed in her seat.

I grabbed the bottle from her and replaced it with a glass of water.

She took a sip, frowned, stared at it, and shrugged before going back to drinking.

I blew out a breath of relief.

"She had too much to drink?" Jaron asked.

"Yeah," I answered. "She usually drinks wine, so I guess beer is hitting her harder."

"How are you getting home?"

My head whipped around. I frowned. "Why?"

Jaron's jaw clenched. "I want to make sure you girls get home safely. I know you don't live near here."

"Obviously," I threw back at him. "We rented a cheap hotel for the night and will head back there after here. Alone," I added.

"Aww." Sunny whispered something in Meadow's ear. "Too bad."

"Well …" She grabbed her phone off the top of the table. "What's your phone number?" she asked, placing her feet on the other man's lap who sat beside them.

Sunny took her phone from her, pressed a couple of buttons, then handed it back.

"Perfect." She gave him a wink.

The longer time went on, the more anxious I became. The guys flirted and talked to Meadow, Gigi was trying hard not to pass out on top of the table, and Jaron kept rubbing his thumb back and forth on my arm. I wished I wasn't wearing just a tank top and shorts. I wished I wasn't there but then, at the same time, happy that I was.

But I needed to get out of there. I needed to take a breath and think before I begged Jaron to come back to my place.

Rising to my feet, I mumbled an excuse and hightailed it to the bathroom. I needed to put some distance between Jaron and me. I needed … God, who was I kidding? I needed *him*.

Paris ruined me. Nothing had ever compared to our night together, but I still left him in the morning. Why? Why the hell did I do that? Because he scared me. My feelings for him scared me. Everything scared me. God, I was losing my mind.

*Tears rolled down my cheeks. I couldn't believe I had fallen off my bike in front of the boys. God, how embarrassing.*

*"Piper."*

*I sniffed, glancing up, and found Jaron hovering over me.*

*"Are you okay?"*

*The tears only poured harder at his question.*

*He sighed, crouching in front of me. "Let me see."*

*I stuck out my leg.*

*"Where does it hurt?"*

*"Everywhere." I pouted.*

*He chuckled. Wrapping a hand around my calf, he bent my knee.*

*A small gasp escaped me at the warmth rushing through me.*

*"Does that hurt?" His eyes popped to mine, his brows narrowing.*

*I quickly shook my head. If anything, he made it feel better.*

*Much to my surprise, he leaned over and placed a soft peck on my knee. "Better?" he asked, glancing up at me.*

*The only thing I could do was sit there and stare. What just happened? Jaron kissed my knee. Jaron Mercer. Just wait until I tell the girls this.*

The memory hit me fast. We had been just kids but that was when my crush for him strengthened. I had always had a tiny one on him before that moment, but when he checked to make sure I was okay, even though his friends would probably give him a hard time about it later, it sealed the deal for how I felt about him. But we had been kids. Nothing could come of our relationship. Could it?

Once I reached the bathroom, I started pacing. I could do this. I could be in the same room as Jaron without wanting to jump him. I could be civil and not make a complete fool of myself. I had this.

With my back to the door, the hairs on my nape tingled. A breath left me as a shadow loomed over me. This was it. This was what I wanted even though I had denied myself that right to just feel.

In a quick move, Jaron spun me and crushed his mouth to mine.

I sighed, taking his tongue deep between my lips. Circling my arms around his shoulders, I dug my fingers into his hair and forced him down harder on my mouth.

He groaned, cupped my ass, and lifted me before carrying me into one of the stalls. Kicking the door closed, he slammed me up against it.

I whimpered, deepening the kiss. He tasted like beer and spice, like he had chased a shot before meeting me in the bathroom.

Placing me on my feet, he released my mouth and spun me around.

Reaching a hand up, I touched my mouth. My lips tingled from his rough kiss.

"It's been a long five weeks without this pussy wrapped around my cock, Piper." His deep voice slid over me, promising me endless orgasms.

"You've kept count?" I asked, shocked that he would even care.

"Of course." He trailed his hand down my side. "I've dreamt of you ever since."

"I'm sure you had other pussy to satisfy you in the meantime," I told him, pushing my ass back into his waist. The bulge in his jeans hinted at how much he was ready for me.

"Nah, baby." Jaron fisted my hair, tugging my head back, and sunk his teeth into the side of my neck. "You see, your pussy is like a damn drug. I had it once, and I want more. I would have had more too but you left."

I swallowed hard at the anger hidden in his voice. "I have no idea what you're talking about."

Jaron pushed my face up against the door with his arm pressed against the back of my neck. "No?" With nimble fingers, he undid the button of my shorts and pushed them down to just below my ass. "You have no idea what I'm talking about? How about I remind you then."

The clanking of his belt sent a nervous flutter racing through me.

"Stick that ass out for me," he demanded, landing a hard swat on my rear.

I whimpered, arching into him.

"That's it. So fucking drenched too, baby." His fingers brushed over my wet center before delving lower to my swollen clit.

A shot of electricity raced up my spine.

"Nice and hard." Jaron pinched the bundle of nerves. "This tiny clit is begging for me to bite it. Isn't it?"

I gasped.

"Tell me who's been inside this body since me."

I couldn't answer. If I did, he would have even more control. The truth was, I didn't want anyone else. Jaron ruined me. That night in Paris destroyed me. And I found although he terrified me, I still wanted more.

"Tell me, Piper," he growled, pushing my face against the door. "Tell me who the fuck has been inside this body since me." He pinched my clit harder.

"No one," I cried out, a fast release hitting me.

"You're lying." Jaron released my clit and slammed his cock into me. "Aren't you?"

I swallowed a scream, meeting him thrust for violent thrust. "I'm not," I whined.

His assault on my body did nothing for the assault he was conducting on my heart.

"So fucking good." Digging his fingers into my hips, he powered into me. "Fuck, Piper, you have the tightest pussy ever. So hot. So wet." He groaned. "Did you miss my cock?"

"Yes," I whispered, slapping my hands against the door and pushing back.

"I bet you did. Did you think of me this whole time?"

I did. God, did I ever think of him. I pushed him back hard, forcing him to fall from my body, and turned around. "I did, Jaron." I pulled my shorts down my legs, leaving me in my wedges and tank top. "I thought of you when I touched myself. When I slid my fingers into my body. When I stroked my throbbing clit. I thought of you the whole fucking time."

His eyes darkened, a smirk spreading on his face. In a quick move, he was on me. With his mouth fused to mine and his hands in my hair, he fucked his way back into my body.

"Jaron," I whispered against his lips. "Please."

Leaning his forehead against mine, he held my head in place and picked up speed with his hips. "Come for me."

Our breathing picked up. The scent of sex wafted around us. It was perfect. It was ours.

"Please." I gripped his jacket, lifted my leg higher around his waist, and took him deeper.

"Fuck, baby." He shivered.

"Harder." I couldn't take it. The pleasure. It was almost too much. He felt so damn good. I wanted more. "Please, Jaron."

"You're so fucking greedy, Piper." He reached between us, strumming my clit.

I jumped, grabbing his hand. My body was oversensitive. I couldn't handle it.

"Don't." He fisted my hair. "You're going to come and you're going to come hard. You're also going to walk out of here with my cum between your thighs and my scent on your skin."

"Yes, please." I was hungry for it. For him. "Harder. Please fuck me harder."

A wicked grin spread on his face. His thumb rubbed my clit. "Come, Piper."

I moaned, rocking against him. "Faster."

Jaron kissed my forehead. "Come for me."

My body shook, my thighs trembling. A release rocked through me, pleasure exploding until stars danced in my vision. His name left my lips on a whisper when I really wanted to scream out how good he was making me feel. But I didn't. I couldn't. Because no one knew that he was fucking me. No one knew that we had sex in Paris. No one knew that I spent most of my life having a crush on him.

And no one knew that I would leave him. Again.

# TWO

*Piper*

**JARON LEANED AGAINST** the wall, watching me while I put my shorts back on and made myself look somewhat presentable.

"You're beautiful," he said, running his fingers through his beard.

I paused. "Y-you think I'm beautiful?"

He nodded. "Why do you seem surprised?"

I wasn't sure. He hadn't really given me compliments before. It was always crude. Not that I ever complained, of course.

"I want to see you again."

I laughed, doing up my shorts. "Right." He wasn't a guy who dated and there was no way I was ready for that shit. I had heard stories of what my parents went through when they were our age. My dad had been a dick and pushed my mom away when she needed him most. I didn't want that for myself.

Jaron closed the distance between us and pinched my chin. "I don't suggest doubting me right now."

"Or else what, Jaron? You got what you wanted. You can leave and head back to the city."

"I'm in town for a few more days, Piper." He tilted my head back. "I *will* see you again."

Shoving my head out of his grip, I left the stall. "Unlikely."

"What the fuck is your problem? I didn't see you pushing me away a moment ago when I was balls deep inside your soaked pussy."

I spun on Jaron, my stomach doing a flip as his cum dripped out of me. Ignoring it, I glared at him. "You know this could never work."

"I'm not fucking proposing to you, Piper. I want sex. I want a lot of sex. And your pussy is the tightest, snuggest one I have ever felt. And it tastes so mother fucking good that I'm addicted. Or is one cock not enough for you?" he asked, raising an eyebrow.

My blood burned through me at what he was implying. "I have no idea what you're talking about."

"No?" He crossed his arms under his chest. "Let me rehash it for you then. Aiden and Ashton. Twins. You get drunk one night and are stuffed with both of their cocks. Does that sound about right?"

Clenching my jaw, I stomped past him when he grabbed my arm. "Why do you fucking care?"

"You see, Piper. I don't care." Jaron kissed my head. "I don't give a shit who you fuck because I know you will always come crawling back to me."

He was lying. He had to have been. There was no way a guy like Jaron would ever share willingly.

Pulling from his rough grip, I stormed out of the washroom and headed to where Meadow and Gigi sat.

They both looked up and stood.

"Sorry, boys. It's girl time." Meadow kissed both men's cheeks she had been flirting with for the past half hour. "I'll call you."

Without having to tell them, we left the bar. Much to the other bikers' dismay, of course.

Jaron's words hurt. They cut deep because they were true. After a drunken binge, I was subjected to a delicious threesome, and with twins no less. But it wasn't enough. It had never been enough, so I couldn't stop sleeping with them. And then Paris happened, and I ended things with the twins.

I hurt them even though it was supposed to be a one-time thing. My life was a mess, and tonight made it worse.

My heart couldn't afford to get caught up with Jaron. I couldn't take it. But he had felt good. So damn good and I wanted more. I would always want more.

And that scared the shit out of me.

# THREE

## JARON

**I STARED DOWN** at Piper while I was deep inside her. Her cheeks were flushed. Her eyes bright and wild with lust. She gave as good as she got. My back was tender with the scratches she had given me.

Ever since we were kids, I had felt the need to protect her. I wasn't sure why. And once I found out she was sleeping with the twins by one of the twins himself, it took everything inside of me not to drive my fist through his face.

But now, here we were. In Paris. Back at my hotel. Wrapped around each other.

Sitting back on my heels, I pulled Piper up with me.

Her body slid farther down my aching cock forcing a soft sigh to escape her mouth. She was so damn beautiful.

Running my hands down the length of her spine, I took it slow, not wanting this moment between us to end any time soon.

I made sure to memorize every inch of her. Her smell. Her taste. The way she felt. Her hands gripping my shoulders, her dark hair framing her beautiful face.

*I placed a soft peck on a freckle on the side of her tit. "You're so fucking incredible," I whispered, wrapping my lips around her nipple.*

*She shivered.*

*At this point, I knew. She was mine. Even though we were in another country and would have to deal with real life shit once we got home, I would make it my sole mission in life to have her at my side.*

That night so many weeks ago had sealed the deal for me. Piper Michaels was my weakness, and I wouldn't have it any other way. But the man sitting across from me knew that.

Price Davies was the mayor of this shithole town Piper and a few of my closest friends called home. I was thankful I grew up in the city even though it wasn't much better.

"What do you want, Price?" I asked the older man. He was pushing fifty but looked more like sixty thanks to the alcohol and drugs he consumed. He had called this meeting but was dragging it out, and it was starting to piss me off.

"You know what I want." Price sat back in the chair he planted his fat ass in and tented his fingers under his chin. The chair creaked beneath his weight, his protruding gut hitting the edge of the table.

"I have unfinished business here." And a tight hot pussy to fill. Over and over again. I wasn't ready to leave without having Piper at least once more. Fuck that woman and what she did to me. So sweet. So damn perfect. So everything that I wasn't.

"Which pussy are you sniffing around?" Price chuckled, glancing around us. "I bet it's one of those kids whose mamas are with that biker gang."

"They're not a gang," I bit out. "It's a club. And who I'm sniffing around is none of your damn business. That's not why we're here." My sex life was off limits. I never kissed and told. Much like Piper, I kept my shit to myself. But when Ashton got drunk the last time I saw the twins and he spilled all, I made it my secret mission to search her out. She just didn't know that.

"There *is* someone." Price smirked. "Isn't there?"

"Listen, old man." I held my anger in check before I punched the mayor out. "Tell me what the fuck we're doing here and why you insisted on this meeting."

"I want you out of my town." Price snapped his fingers, signaling the waitress over. "Beer for me and get him whatever he wants."

"Nothing for me," I told the young girl who was probably no older than sixteen. Girls like her were why we were actually in this town. "Thank you."

She nodded, spinning on her heel, but not before Price smacked her hard on the ass. She jumped, shooting him a glare.

He raised an eyebrow, daring her to say something.

But she was smart and didn't. It was sad, really. Men like him should be shot and pissed on. And that would be something we would do. Once we had proof, of course. Word on the street was that the mayor and his son, Brody, were running a company in the porn industry and this club was just a ruse. I was a supporter of porn. Whatever tickled your fancy and shit. But when it came to barely-legal girls that was when I decided to take action and shut this shit down.

I was an asshole, but I never touched something that didn't belong to me. *Piper.*

My dick stirred. Fuck. She wasn't mine. At all. No. She belonged to the twins. As much as I didn't like it, I couldn't blame them.

"Does she hang out with my son?" Price asked, scanning the area around us. He was like a disease, latching on to anything and everything.

"Who's your son?" It wouldn't surprise me if Brody Davies hung out with Piper and her friends. It was a small town. Everyone grew up together and were almost forced to become friends whether they liked it or not.

"Like you don't know." Price crossed his arms under his chest which lifted the bottom of his shirt even more, causing more of his protruding gut to appear.

I *did* know, but like a good little boy, I played dumb. "I have no idea what you're talking about."

"Right." Price rolled his eyes. "And your father isn't Greyson Mercer. Oh and the rest of the club you're in isn't tailing this place or just … hanging out." He used air quotes for that last part.

My jaw clenched but I kept my face impassive. There would be no way I would let this bastard know anything about my life. He only knew what he was told which was exactly what we had wanted.

"Again, I have no idea what you're talking about." I moved to stand when his next words stopped me.

"I suggest leaving this town before things get really ugly. You wouldn't want your little girlfriend and her friends to get hurt, would you?"

"Is that a threat?" I growled. Bodies shifted around us, my men finally coming out in the open. Although my father was the president, I was the VP and he left me in charge when needed. He was also on the verge of retiring and making me president instead, so this was a test. And it was a test that I would win no matter who I had to kill in the process. I didn't give a shit if the bastard sitting across from me was the mayor of this fucked up town. We would get the proof we needed to bring him, his son, and whoever else was involved down. We may have done some shady shit in the past, but we would never harm children or animals. And if we found out one of our club brothers was abusive to their partner, we made them disappear.

"No." Price rubbed the smattering of scruff on his jaw. "It's a promise. Make sure you leave quietly too."

I sat back in my chair just as the waitress returned with his drink.

"Thank you, sweetheart." He grabbed her arm before she could pull away. "How about you come visit me in about ten minutes. I would like to order more drinks and maybe some of your services."

"I'm not a whore," she said through clenched teeth.

"You work here. You're a whore. Now leave us." He released her roughly before turning back to me.

She shot me a look, almost pleading for me to help her.

I would, but not yet. The piece of trash sitting across from me would get his. I guaranteed it.

"To answer your question, Jaron." The mayor sat forward. "Your club, as you call it, is fucking things up for me. I'm running for office again, as you know, so I need to keep this town clean. You guys being here is not helping."

I bit back a scoff. We weren't the problem.

"We're not doing anything. I also have family here. There's no law that says we have to leave." I sat back in the chair, crossing my arms under my chest.

"No." Price rubbed his jaw. "But I need to make it look good, and besides your family and friends, there's nothing here for you."

My family and friends were all I needed to make an appearance in this shithole town. I didn't need any other reason to visit.

"So, I suggest leaving. And soon too because I will know if you don't." Price took a long swig of his beer.

"You going to have Brody watching?"

"I thought you didn't know who my son is?" Price waved a hand in front of him. "Either way, it doesn't matter. Yes, Brody will be watching and report back to me. You're not stupid. You'd know that even before I told you."

My jaw clenched. I hated being told what to do. It pissed me off to the extreme. I got that trait from my father. He wasn't known as a hothead for no reason.

Bodies shifted around us, waiting for their instructions.

"So, what will it be, Jaron?" Price raised an eyebrow. "You going to be a good boy and listen to me for once?"

I stood, resting my knuckles on the tabletop, and peered into Price's eyes. "You're lucky you're the mayor of this shitty town."

"Yeah?" His brows narrowed. "Or else what?"

I sneered. "You've heard the stories about my father. I'm worse. So much fucking worse than him. Believe it or not, Mr. Mayor." I moved behind him, his men shifting and watching to make sure I wouldn't do anything stupid. I leaned down, fixing the collar of his shirt. "You won't always have your men with you."

I left the club with my men following right behind me. I needed air. My hands clenched into fists.

"Hey." Cyrus came toward me with his twin brother hot on his heels. He lit up a smoke and handed it to his brother before lighting another one for himself. "What did the mayor say?"

Needing to get out of earshot, in case anyone happened to be listening in, I headed to my bike that sat at the outer edge of the parking lot. Turning to the twins, I nodded to the other guys that had joined me during my meeting with the mayor. "You can leave," I told them. They revved their engines and left me alone with the twins, knowing I was safe and well protected. I was the president's son and all.

"He wants us out of town," I told the twins.

"Are you going to leave?" Sammy asked.

I grunted. "Fuck no. He can't do shit all. Doesn't matter that he's the mayor."

"Did you find out anything else?" Cyrus asked, puffing on his smoke.

"No." I glanced back at the club. "But I would bet on my fucking life that most of those girls are underage. I think the club is a front."

Sammy cursed. "I don't understand these fuckers who get off on little girls."

"Neither do I, but we also have no proof." And it pissed me off.

"You should lay low for a few days," Cyrus suggested. "Aren't your friends throwing a party next week?"

"Probably. Gigi always throws parties." Just like my father. It was distracting in a way. So I got it.

"Alright." Cyrus butted out his smoke on the bottom of his boot. "So lay low. We'll see if we can find out some more info."

"Yes," Sammy added. "And we'll report back to you."

I nodded. "Fine."

"Maybe you can go meet up with that hot little thing you were drooling over a week ago." Sammy waggled his eyebrows.

I smacked him across the head. "Leave her out of this."

"I'm just joking, fucker." He rubbed the spot I hit, his dark eyes flashing with amusement.

"Does she need protecting?" Cyrus asked, ignoring his brother's playfulness.

"If Brody, the mayor's son, is friends with them like I'm assuming he is, yes. They all do." I didn't like that I couldn't protect Piper myself but that would come in time. Cyrus was right; I had to lay low. And even though that would be hard for me to do, I would hole up in our motel room. For now.

## (Piper)

It was finally Saturday night. Gigi was throwing a party and I was on a mission to get Jaron out of my head. Even though it had been only a week since the bar incident, it had felt like forever since I had seen him.

I found out that he hadn't left town like he said he would. I only knew that thanks to my friends keeping tabs on him. But I also knew that if he didn't want me to know he was still around, I wouldn't. We didn't grow up in the biker world like he had. Although our moms were part of a club, they kept us out of it and us girls had no interest in being part of that life anyway.

Unlike Jaron who was every bit a biker as his father was and the rest of the guys in his club.

My body hummed, remembering the scent of his leather cut. My fingers tingled, itching to touch him. Just once, I would love to spend the night with him where it was gentle. Not that I complained when he took full control and used me good and hard, but I wanted to know what it felt like to make love to him. *Love*. I bit back a scoff. Please.

Letting out a sigh, I scanned the items in front of me. I wasn't even sure why I was at the store. Oh, right. Ice. And anything else I could think of for Gigi's party.

My thoughts traveled back to Jaron. I didn't know what business he had in town, but he became broody. Everywhere I went, I could feel him watching me. I didn't know why or how. Maybe I was losing my mind. How could I let a guy affect me this way? My parents taught me better. My mom especially.

"Piper."

I jumped, spinning around, and found Aiden and Ashton Donovan coming toward me. Great. Just what I needed. Two more men to give me a hard time.

"How's it going?" Aiden asked, pushing a loose strand of hair behind my ear. His piercing blue eyes bore into mine. He was the quiet one. Compassionate and kind. While Ashton was the jokester and partier, Aiden liked to keep to himself. But it still didn't stop either of them from touching me whenever they felt like it.

I shivered, taking a step back. "It's going fine."

Aiden frowned, his gaze slicing through me. I had called off our fling, but it didn't mean the twins never tried to get me back in bed.

"I leave on Monday." Aiden nodded at his brother. "Ashton will take care of you while—"

"No," I snapped. "I mean … I'm going to miss you." I took a breath.

His eyes softened.

"Of course I'm going to miss you but this—" I waved a hand between us "—I told you it was over."

"I know." Aiden glanced at his brother. "He's still going to watch you."

"You can't stop me," Ashton added.

Ignoring him, I headed back down the aisle. Aiden was being shipped out on his first leave after joining the Navy like our fathers. I would miss him. It would be hard not to but a part of me was thankful he wouldn't be in town to press me for more. They wanted what I couldn't give them. I never led them on, and I told them exactly what I wanted in the beginning, but it never stopped them from flirting.

I continued walking down the aisle, forgetting why I had come to the grocery store in the first place. Ice. Right. *God, get it together, Piper.*

"Why are you walking away from this?" Ashton asked, following me.

"You know why. I told you guys that I'm done." I felt guilty enough for fucking Jaron in Paris while I was still sleeping with the twins. Even though we never made anything official, it still wasn't right of me.

"Whether you like it or not, I'll be around, Piper." Ashton grabbed a case of beer from the bottom shelf. "We'll see you at the party." He leaned down to my ear. "You'll beg for more. They always do." He kissed my cheek and headed to the cash register.

Aiden followed his brother but not before he gave me a look.

I swallowed hard, turning away. As much as I didn't like to admit it, Ashton was right. I *had* begged for more but that was before Jaron showed up in Paris. That was before I followed him back to his hotel room and spent the night in his bed. That was before I gave my heart to a guy who wanted nothing more than sex. It wasn't Jaron's fault. He never led me on. It was just my heart getting in the way of me actually enjoying myself for once.

Did the twins know I had slept with someone else? I never gave them a reason when I ended things. I just said I was finished. It wasn't good enough for them, but I refused to give them more. I cared for them deeply and didn't want to hurt them in any way but when they started judging because they were pissed, my sympathy simmered.

Letting out a hard sigh, I grabbed a shopping cart and filled it with bags of ice before I forgot again. Once I paid, I headed to my car only to find Jaron leaning against it.

I stopped in my tracks, the tiny hairs on my body tingling under his intense scrutiny.

He crooked his finger, indicating for me to go to him and, like a good little girl, I did.

Jaron smirked.

If I wasn't carrying the bags of ice, I would have smacked that smirk right off of his handsome face.

Without saying anything, he came toward me and grabbed the bags from my hands.

"What are you doing here?" I asked him, unlocking the trunk to my car.

"I told you I wanted to see you again." He placed the bags in the back and closed the trunk.

I looked around us.

"Don't worry. The twins are gone." Jaron took the keys from my hand and opened the passenger side door.

"What are you doing?" I didn't know what his intentions were. Just sex?

"I'm holding the door open for you." His brows narrowed. "I'm being a gentleman. Don't make me regret it."

I swallowed hard at the threat in his voice. "Fine. I was just asking a question." I slid into the vehicle. "You don't have to be a dick."

He chuckled, shutting me into the car.

Letting out a hard sigh, I wiped my sweaty hands down my thighs.

Once Jaron was seated beside me, he laughed.

"What?" I frowned.

"It's funny." He shook his head, his gaze sliding to mine. "I've never had a woman question me when I tell them I want to see them again."

"Have you ever seen the same woman more than once? Aren't you a fuck 'em and leave 'em kind of guy?" I crossed my arms under my chest, lifting my chin. "Or is my pussy just that good?"

The smile fell from his face. In a quick move, he grabbed my right arm and pulled me against him.

"Sass me again, Piper." His grip on my arm tightened.

"Let go of me." I struggled against him, but he only spun me around so I was facing the back seat of the car.

"Do it," he growled, lifting my dress to my waist.

"Fuck you," I bit out through clenched teeth.

His hand landed against my ass.

I yelped, the burn from his palm spreading over me.

"Do it," he repeated, his mouth brushing over my ear. "Sass me."

My body heated at the mere intensity of lust in his gray eyes. "Fuck. You."

His lips twitched, his palm connecting with my rear once again. "Again."

"Fuck," I panted. "You."

Swat. Swat. Swat.

An unexpected moan escaped me. I was shocked at myself, never knowing I liked any amount of pain. The twins were dominant but nothing like Jaron.

"Again." Jaron's hot breath fanned the side of my face.

"Fuck you," I whispered.

Swat.

Spots danced in my vision, a soft gasp escaping me.

"Hmm …" Jaron rubbed his hand over my ass cheek. "I can't wait for the day I get to play with that little masochist inside of you." He kissed my temple. "Now tell me you don't want me again." He released my arm. "Tell me that this pussy isn't soaked right now. Tell me you're not aching to be filled by my cock."

My core clenched, my thoughts racing over what just happened.

"Say it, Piper," Jaron demanded, his voice rough.

"Take me home." I sat back on the seat, my ass sensitive from the many times he spanked me, but it only seemed to heighten the desire I had for him.

His steel eyes moved over my face. "You're a fucking challenge, baby." He sat back, put the car into gear, and drove us through my small town.

Should I have been ashamed over what happened? Maybe if it were with anyone else I would have been, but with Jaron it was almost like I expected it.

Once we pulled onto my street, cars lined one side. When Gigi threw a party, she invited half the town, which usually ended up stressing out our fathers but, thankfully, they stopped randomly dropping by.

When we reached the house I lived in with Gigi, Meadow, and Luna, we ended up driving by it instead.

My head whipped around. "What are you doing?"

"Driving." Jaron pulled his cell out of the inside of his jacket.

"Why aren't you taking me home?" What the hell was going on?

"We have a problem," he said to whoever was on the other end of the phone. "Yes. I'm with her. Yup. Thanks, man." He hung up and put his cell away.

"What's going on?" I asked, my heart racing. "Jaron." I punched his arm when he didn't answer. "Tell me."

"There's someone at your house who shouldn't be."

"That doesn't tell me anything. Who were you on the phone with? How did they know that you're with me?" I let out a frustrated cry when he didn't respond. "Jaron. Please."

He grabbed my hand, bringing it up to his mouth. "Do you trust me?" He kissed my fingertips.

"I …" My heart jumped. "I don't know."

"Why?" he asked, pushing his thumb into the palm of my hand.

"B-because you're dangerous for my health." If we weren't in a moving vehicle, I would have climbed him right there. Screw my health.

He winked, releasing my hand. "Are you friends with the mayor's son?"

"Brody? Yeah." I frowned. "Why?"

"Can you trust him?" Jaron cupped my inner thigh, but he didn't hint for more.

I blew out a slow breath, thankful for that. "We trust him. We've known him for years. You would know that if you actually came around once in a while."

"Careful, Piper." He released my inner thigh. "I'll spank that ass again until my handprint is permanently embedded on your fucking skin."

I shivered at the thought.

He chuckled, leaning against the door, and rubbed the beard on his strong jaw.

"You're an asshole," I muttered.

"I am but you keep coming back for more." Clearing his throat, he glanced my way. "Listen, Brody isn't a good guy. You can't trust him. And as much as it pisses me off, I can't be seen by him either."

I frowned. "Why not?"

"Because we're not supposed to be in town. According to his father, anyway."

"How come?" I turned toward him, leaning against the door. "Were you a bad boy?"

"Not overly, but I did fuck Brody's fiancée, and apparently he didn't like that too much." Jaron shrugged like it was no big deal.

"That was you?" I exclaimed. "He came over that night and got shit-faced with the twins, complaining about some asshole his fiancée had sex with. But he never mentioned your name."

"His girl did." Jaron grinned. "Over and over again."

"When was this?" I tried doing the math in my head.

"That was before Paris." He cupped my center. "Don't worry. Nothing beats this pussy, and I haven't been with anyone since."

I scoffed, finding that hard to believe.

"You don't believe me?"

"Why should I?" I grabbed his hand, removing it from between my legs. "You've said that my pussy is the only one you want and yet it's been a week since the bar and this is the first time I'm seeing you. Why?"

"I've had to lay low for a few days. I wasn't lying when I said that the mayor wants us out of town. Besides, why do you care? Are you wanting a relationship?"

"What?" My cheeks burned. "I never said that. I just … I …" I huffed.

"Look, I know you've been with the twins for a while. I'm not stupid and people talk. So I figured you're not ready for a relationship. Am I ready? I have no fucking idea. But I do know that I want sex and a lot of it."

"You said that already." I stared out the window.

"It's the truth."

"Sex is dangerous," I murmured.

"Yeah, baby. It can be." He linked his fingers in mine, holding my hand in my lap.

My heart jumped at the gentle touch. Especially coming from him. "What are we doing?"

"Fucking." He squeezed my hand. "It's just sex, Piper. I know you can handle that. You did it with the twins."

The twins were different. I didn't feel for them what I felt for Jaron, but those feelings terrified me. He could break my heart.

"I broke it off after Paris," I confessed. "I felt guilty even though I wasn't committed to them."

"You shouldn't feel guilty. You weren't in a relationship."

"Maybe." I brushed my thumb over the back of his hand. His tanned skin was a contradiction to my pale form. "Why did we wait until Paris?"

"Because you were fucking Aiden and Ashton. Or I guess they were fucking you."

"No." I leaned my head against the window. "*You* fuck me. They … they weren't dominant like you are."

"They didn't please your tasty pussy, Piper? Is that what you're saying to me?"

"Why do you have to make everything dirty or crude?" I pushed his hand out of my lap and faced the front.

"You like it. That's why." Jaron grabbed my hand.

"Stop." I shoved out of his grip.

"Don't fucking push me away, Piper." He cupped my hand. "We may only be fucking but you belong to me. You aren't satisfied by anything else. Isn't that right?"

"Where are you taking me?" I asked, instead of answering him.

"To my aunt and uncle's place. I need to talk to them about Brody and find out what they know."

"What they know?" I knew Coby and Brogan Porter used to be informants in a way. If that was what you could even call them. But as far as I knew, they were retired.

"Yeah, Piper." Jaron brushed his thumb back and forth over my palm. "I remember when you got this scar," he said, running his thumb over the soft pink line that was slashed across my palm.

I laughed as the memories rushed forth. "Me too. I was trying to impress you and the guys," I confessed.

He chuckled. "I think it worked. For me anyway." He winked.

I gave him a small smile, my cheeks burning. "I also remember all of our parents freaking out. I think my dad was more upset than my mom."

"Well you did cut yourself on glass," Jaron reminded me.

"True." I turned to him, curling my leg under me. "You guys all did it first." They had broken beer bottles against something hard, trying to be cool. I did the same and ended up cutting myself. "But I didn't cry."

"I think that's what impressed me most."

I shrugged. "I'm not a crier."

"No." He cupped my calf. "I guess you aren't."

### (Jaron)

She was difficult and driving me fucking crazy. But I found that I liked it. Although I had said it was just sex, both of us knew that it was more than that.

Cyrus and Sammy couldn't find any more information than we already knew. The mayor was good at covering his tracks. I had to give him that.

As my fingers linked with Piper's, I couldn't help but wonder what would come of this. Piper wasn't easy like most of the women I had been with. Even though it didn't take long to get her into my bed when we were in Paris, she sure as hell wasn't letting me into her heart. Did I want her to? I wasn't sure anymore, but I did know that I would fuck her for as long as both of us needed.

Aiden and Ashton wouldn't get in the way. No matter what I had to do, she would be mine.

Again.

# FOUR

*Piper*

**"BROGAN'S RETIRED. THEY** both are. Aren't they?" Our parents didn't talk much about what they did before us kids were born but stories went around about Brogan and Coby. She was a bad ass when she was our age. But that was all we knew.

"Doesn't matter," Jaron said. "I need to talk to them because I need them to watch over all of you. They'll talk to Creena and Stone and they'll do the same thing. Until I can figure this shit out about Brody."

"What has Brody done to make you leery of him?"

"Nothing we've been able to prove yet," Jaron muttered.

"Were you watching me this whole time?" I asked him as we pulled down a gravel road. I realized then that we were no longer in town.

"I was, or I had someone else watching you. But either way, you were being watched."

"Why?" This side of Jaron threw me off. I wasn't sure how to take it, but I knew that if he kept this up, I could fall, and I could fall damn hard. Oh, who the hell was I kidding? I had already fallen.

"I had to make sure you were okay when I wasn't around." He shrugged. "That's the truth, Piper. You can take it however you want."

"Why would you care what happens to me? If this is just sex and all." The car suddenly came to a complete stop and the next thing I knew, I was back in Jaron's arms.

"Say that to me again," he growled, inching his hands beneath the hem of my dress.

"You told me it was just sex." I brushed my thumb over his bottom lip. "Is that not correct? Were you worried that something would happen to me? Do you actually care about me, Jaron?"

With a tug, he snapped the sides of my panties. "I like you, Piper. Is it just sex? You bet your sweet ass it is because I know that's all either of us can handle right now. But yes, I care about you. Of course I care about you. Paris fucked me up. It fucked me up in ways I never knew were possible. You're the first woman I've ever continued sleeping with."

"We haven't done much sleeping." I shivered, enjoying the feel of his rough calloused hands on my lower body.

"No. I guess we haven't." His eyes moved back and forth over my face. He stared. He stared to the point I could feel him reaching into my soul and finding out all of my dark and dirty secrets. Secrets that I wanted to share with only him.

"Have you fucked anyone else?" I murmured, running my fingers through his hair.

"No."

I leaned back, raising an eyebrow. "You're serious, aren't you?"

"I don't give a shit if you believe me or not. Before you, I had pussy lined up and ready to bounce on my dick, but it's not my thing anymore since you introduced me to your cunt." He brought my panties between us, swiping his thumb over the crotch of it. "So no, I have not fucked anyone else, Piper."

My body buzzed.

"Looks like our moment earlier really turned you on." His gaze locked with mine. "I never pegged you for someone who likes pain."

"Neither did I," I whispered, my eyes widening when he brought the ripped fabric of my thong up to his nose and inhaled.

A soft rumble left his chest.

"I don't mean to be rude, but I find this very hard to believe," I said, needing to distract myself. "And if you don't want a relationship, what the hell are we doing? We're only fucking each other. Isn't that a relationship?"

Jaron unbuckled his belt and pulled out his swollen cock.

My mouth watered.

He chuckled. "Hop on, baby."

"We're in the middle of no—" Jaron lifted me to my knees and dropped me down the length of him.

I sighed, a low moan escaping the back of my throat.

"Fucking perfect." He kept his arm around me, thrusting his hips up and down. "Shit, I can't get enough of this tight pussy."

"Jaron," I whined, trying to move but his hold on me was too strong. He was in full control as he fucked me hard and deep.

"Do you love the twins? Do you miss being with them?"

"What?" I asked, my eyes widening.

"Do you love them?" he asked, in between thrusts. "I need to know, Piper. They're competition. If they weren't my friends, I would have taken them out already."

"Why are you asking me this now?"

"Because you're in the most vulnerable position, Piper." Jaron lowered me at the same time as he pushed into me.

I gasped for breath at how deep he was inside me. "I can't ..." I shivered.

"Tell me." He pinched my chin, forcing me to look at him. "Do you love them?"

"No," I whined, struggling against him. He either needed to move or stop this shit. It fucked with my head. I couldn't handle him.

"Tell me why you ended it. Why you really ended it."

Something inside of me snapped. I grabbed his hands from my hips and lifted myself off his cock before slamming back down.

He shouted out, his eyes rolling into the back of his head.

"I ended it because they don't compare to you," I told him, circling my fingers in his. "I don't want a relationship. I did that shit with them and it fucked me up. Is that what you want to hear, Jaron? You want to hear how all this time, even before them, I craved sex. I needed it and even both of their cocks couldn't do anything." I leaned forward, licking along his bottom lip. "But your cock is bigger."

"Fuck," he breathed.

"Fatter." I sunk my teeth into his lip. "I've never come so damn hard."

A wicked grin spread on his face. "My cock is all that you'll ever crave." Fisting my hair, he tugged my head back and thrust up and up. "This pussy won't come unless it's me fucking it. Isn't that right, Piper?"

I swallowed hard. I wanted him to stop. To just make me come and leave me alone. But I couldn't stop myself. One look from him and I was panting at his feet, begging him to do whatever he pleased to me. It was never like this with the twins. Although what we had wasn't conventional, it was far more vanilla than what I shared with Jaron. All he had to do was talk to me and flash those sexy as hell dimples and I was done.

"Come, Piper. Squirt this sweet honey all over me." Jaron started stroking my clit.

The pleasure increased, forcing cries from my lips. My body shook. My thighs burned. But I couldn't stop. The pain. It was so fucking good. "More," I whispered, my eyes fluttering closed as the ecstasy shot through me and left my mouth on a scream.

Jaron crushed his mouth against mine, forcing his tongue between my lips and stole the rest of my cries. He took my very breath.

"Fuck, baby." His eyes were dark, billowing with a lust that I craved just the same. "I'm ready to splash my cum against the walls of this pussy."

I shivered, his words so damn vulgar and hot all at the same time.

His body shuddered, his release shooting deep inside me. We didn't use a condom. We never used condoms.

"We don't use condoms," I said, voicing my thoughts.

Sitting up straighter, he cupped my head and stared intently into my eyes. "Do I look like I give a fuck?" His hand brushed over my lower belly. "I know you're on the pill. Aren't you?"

I nodded, my skin tingling under the mere intensity of him.

"Did you use condoms with the twins?"

I laughed, pushing him back, and slid off his dick. "You would like that, wouldn't you?" I left the car, righting my dress and made myself look somewhat presentable before having to face his aunt and uncle.

"Answer the damn question, Piper." Jaron slammed the driver's side door shut, peering at me over the hood of the car. "Tell me."

"That's none of your business," I threw back at him. "You already know too much because Ashton has a big fucking mouth." Whenever he drank, he kissed and told.

"Oh, it is my business, Piper. Especially when my boys are currently swimming inside your tight little body."

"God." I threw my hands up in the air. "Just once I would like to have a normal conversation with you. Do you think we can do that? Huh, Jaron? No. Probably not. Because you have to turn everything around and make it all about you and sex. I like sex. Alright? Thank you for making me feel like a fucking slut by bringing the twins into our shit all the damn time. If you want me to hate you, you're doing a wonderful fucking job of it." I stormed past him and headed in the direction of his aunt and uncle's house. My blood boiled, my heart pounding hard in my ears. Much to my surprise, Jaron didn't fight me. He did run to catch up with me but, other than that, he didn't say anything.

I found that hurt a bit, and I couldn't figure out why. I was confused. So damn confused. I wasn't ready for a relationship, but I also didn't want to fuck anyone else *but* Jaron. It didn't make sense. Add to the fact he wasn't sleeping with anyone else either, and I was a complete mess.

"My uncle can contact a friend about Brody," Jaron eventually said, breaking the silence as we stopped in front of Brogan and Coby's front door. "Find out what his deal is."

"What happened to make you guys not trust him?" I asked him. Was this it? Were we actually having an adult conversation without arguing or fucking?

"His father is into some shady shit. He's a slimy fucker but of course, we haven't been able to pinpoint anything on him. I'll tell you more when I know. I promise." Jaron pushed a strand of hair behind my hair. "With him being the mayor and all, it's been hard but I'm stubborn."

I swayed toward him, a hot shiver racing down my spine at the gentle contact.

"Hmm ..." He licked his full mouth, brushing a finger down the length of my jaw. My skin erupted into tiny goose bumps. "So damn perfect."

"Jaron," I whispered.

He pushed me back, hooking his other arm around my middle and pulling me flush against him. "What you said just now." He kissed the side of my neck. "It's not about me. It's never been about me, Piper."

I swung my arms around his neck, holding him against me. "Then what is it?"

"It's everything. Nothing. It's confusing. I'm confused. Alright?"

My heart stuttered at this side of him I had never seen before. "I'm confused too. I like you. I like you a lot but that scares me. I don't want a relationship. Or ... I don't think I do anyway. But ..."

"Do you want more, Piper?" he asked, cupping my cheek.

"I don't know but I do know that I only want you. That scares me too because I know you could hurt me."

"I would never hurt you, baby," he muttered, pulling me tighter against him. It was so damn tight, it was like he was trying to pull me inside him. It was hard to breathe but I found that I didn't care. This moment, this moment right here with him, was what I needed.

"Maybe not intentionally." I ran my fingers through the hair at his nape. "But you could. I don't think I could handle that."

He lifted his head, staring down at me. "I know you like the twins. Even though you told them it was over, you obviously still care about them."

"I do. I'm not going to lie and say I don't but this … this is different."

"How?"

"Because I don't feel for them what I feel for you," I confessed.

"How do you feel about me?" Jaron asked, his voice lowering. "Tell me, Piper. Tell me everything."

"I—"

Suddenly, the door swung open.

I jumped, pushing away from Jaron, but he only stood there with a cocky smirk on his face. Clearing my throat, I gave myself a shake.

"Hey, guys." Brogan leaned her head out the door. She smiled at both of us. "I thought I heard voices. Come in." She stepped back, holding the door open for us.

I stepped into the house with Jaron following me. My body burned. I turned, giving him a glare. "Stop staring at my ass," I muttered, low enough for only him to hear.

"Can you feel my cum dripping down your inner thighs, Piper? Do you want to wipe it up with your panties that I have in my pocket? No?" He kissed my cheek. "Didn't think so." And with that, he walked farther into the house.

I swore this man was going to give me whiplash. One moment he was sweet and caring, and the next he was a douche. I wasn't sure which part of him I was attracted to more.

"You good?"

My gaze snapped to Brogan's, my cheeks burning. "Uh … yeah."

She shook her head, a soft smile splaying on her face. "Be careful with that one."

"What do you mean?" I followed her to the end of the hall.

"His dad can be an asshole, but Jaron?" She laughed. "Yeah, he's way worse. He'll make a perfect president for their club." She sighed and walked into the living room, leaving me to my own thoughts.

It was odd in a way how we, as kids, saw our parents in a different way than their friends. I never would have guessed that Greyson was an asshole. He had always been nice to me, but I had a feeling that was mostly his wife's doing.

Taking a deep breath, I headed into the living room and found Jaron standing with his uncle. He caught my gaze, something flashing behind his eyes but other than that, his face was impassive.

"Your dad told us that you're not allowed in town," Coby said, sitting at the dining room table. The large man looked pointedly between both Jaron and me. "I have no issues with bikers and what you all do. Skirting the law and shit. Hell, my wife and I …"

Brogan took that moment to sit beside him. "We've played." She laughed. "Those were the days."

Jaron chuckled, sitting at the table across from them. The remaining seat was beside him. He pulled it out and patted the seat.

Making nice, I sat beside him and regretted it the moment his big hand skirted beneath my dress. I grabbed his hand, stopping it from going any higher.

"Brody has been sniffing around my gir … friends," Jaron explained, loosening his hold on my thigh.

My heart jumped. Was he going to say what I thought he was going to say?

"The mayor can't stop us from coming to town," he continued. "But he can make our lives difficult. I met with him recently. I was supposed to bring back info to my dad, but I didn't get anything. Just a threat. But…" Jaron winked at me. "Clearly that threat didn't do much."

"No kidding." Brogan laughed. "You're worse than your father. You get told to do something and you do the complete opposite."

Jaron shrugged. "It's in my blood."

"Doesn't surprise me." Coby rubbed the graying scruff on his strong jaw. "I would do the same thing. But we haven't heard anything. The girls have been focused on The Dove Project." He looked down at his wife. "Have you heard anything, little one?"

"No." Brogan sat back in her chair, crossing her arms under her chest. "You need to be careful though. Brody's a good kid. Do I trust him? No. But I can't see him hurting your …" She winked at me. "Friends."

My cheeks burned. Looking down at my lap, I pulled my dress up to my thighs so I could see Jaron's hand. Was it always like this with him? Would it always be like this? Intense and powerful. All-consuming. I wondered if he could ever be gentle.

As if he could hear my thoughts, he gave my thigh a sharp pinch.

My gaze shot to his.

"I asked you a question," he said, his voice laced with annoyance.

"What?" I snapped.

"Has Brody ever said anything?" Jaron demanded. "Anything at all."

"No. Why would he? That's all his dad. He's said he wants nothing to do with politics." Speaking of, Gigi was probably wondering where the hell I was. "He's at the party tonight. Drive me there and I can listen, to see if he says something or not."

"I don't fucking think so." Jaron turned back around.

"She has a point," Brogan said gently. "Brody won't hurt them. I don't think he has a mean bone in his body."

"Those are the ones you have to watch out for," Jaron muttered. "Do you trust him?" he asked me.

"I …" I paused. I never really thought about it before but now that I did, Brody was kind of odd. "He's awkward." I sat back, crossing my ankle over my knee which made Jaron think he had the invitation to cup my pussy. I waited, thinking he was going to do some taboo shit and finger me in front of his aunt and uncle, but when he didn't, it confused me even more. It was almost like he was letting me know that he owned me in a way. "I can't explain it. Brody gets along with all of us. Maybe he gets along with everyone too well."

"Interesting." Coby stood from the table. "I'll call Lucas," he told his wife, brushing a hand down her cheek. "Meet me in my office when you're done." He glanced our way. "It was good seeing you two. I'll get this shit underway. Any new information, let me know."

Jaron nodded. "I will."

### (Jaron)

I liked her. Fuck, did I ever like her. Piper was everything that I wasn't. She pushed and pulled and took everything I had to give her and more. She made me feel good about myself when I felt worthless half the time. It never made sense when I had a good upbringing. I wasn't abused and all that shit. But I had always felt … off. Like I didn't deserve happiness.

Cyrus and Sammy lost both of their parents at a young age. I almost felt guilty for being happy. It stopped me from embracing anything more than just sex with Piper. It didn't make sense. Not one fucking bit.

Piper and I walked back to her car after leaving my aunt and uncle's place. Knowing I would get the information I was looking for and rather quickly, I wasn't surprised when my phone started vibrating in my pocket.

"Yeah," I answered.

"You're just like your father." Uncle Coby chuckled. "Anyway, my contact couldn't find anything on Price."

"You were able to get information this fast?" Even though I knew he could get information quickly, I still wasn't expecting it so soon.

"I did. My contact is good. Retired, of course. Has to keep his nose clean and shit now that he has a family of his own. Anyway, the mayor is fucking clean. Which doesn't surprise me at all. And Brody's record looks almost *too* clean."

I stopped.

Piper glanced over her shoulder, frowning. She came toward me.

"What do you mean?" I asked my uncle.

"He volunteers, helps others, blah blah fucking blah." He grunted. "If anything, it's like he's hiding something. I've been around long enough to know when something seems too good to be true."

"Could he not just be a good person?" It was unlikely, but I had to ask anyway.

"Not when his father is the way he is. The apple doesn't usually fall far from the tree and shit."

"Did you know Brody volunteers?" I asked Piper.

"He does?" Piper's brows narrowed. "I've never heard him mention anything about volunteering. He usually complains when his dad tries to get him to do stuff like that and he ends up making an excuse to get out of it."

"Did you hear her?" I asked my uncle.

"Yeah. Listen, Jaron, be careful. I know you're like your father and hate being told what to do but if the mayor told you to get out of town, you probably should."

"No." I gripped my phone tightly in my hand. "I get what you're saying but something is off, and I refuse to drive away until I know for sure that Piper and our friends are safe from this shit. Price and Brody are both hiding something. I will find out what it is."

"Alright. That I can't argue with. But please be careful."

"I will." I said goodbye to Uncle Coby and stuffed my cell back into the pocket of my cut.

"What's going on?" Piper asked.

"I'll drive you to Gigi's party." I cupped her cheek.

She covered my hand, leaning into my palm.

My heart stuttered. If I didn't have to find out what the hell was going on, I would take her back to my motel with me. I would spend the night savoring every inch of her. But that wouldn't happen. And a part of me wondered if it would ever happen again.

# FIVE

*Piper*

**ONCE WE LEFT** Brogan and Coby's place, my nerves were shot. I didn't know what the hell was up with Jaron, but I found that I wanted to know more about him. What made him tick. What quirks did he have? Did he leave the cap off the toothpaste? Or did he leave the lights on? My heart picked up speed. I shouldn't want to know these things because I knew while he could be gentle at one moment, he could also be a domineering dick a second later. But why the hell was I so attracted to him?

"What are you thinking about?" Jaron asked, putting the car into park a few houses down from mine.

"Are you like this with all the women you have sex with? Your crudeness and vulgar words?" I took a chance and glanced at him.

"I'm a guy." He shrugged. "We're always crude."

"No." I shook my head. "Not like you."

"Are you complaining?" he asked, his voice lowering.

"I have no idea anymore." I opened the door and went to leave the vehicle when his next words stopped me.

"I like you, Piper. Don't ruin that by asking questions you're not ready to get the answers to."

"Whatever."

"Piper," he said gently.

"What are we doing, Jaron?" I asked, closing the door and turning to him. "I know you said you don't want a relationship. Hell, neither do I but I need to know."

"What do you need to know?" he asked, grabbing my hand. "You need to know that I've thought about you every damn second since Paris? You need to know that I would fight two of my good friends for you? You need to know that no matter what you're wanting, I'm not good enough for you? Add to the fact that both of us keep saying that we're not ready for a relationship but …"

"But we're only sleeping with each other," I added.

He nodded.

"How do you know that you're not good enough for me?" I asked, letting him pull me closer.

"I …" He leaned his forehead against mine, sliding his hand to the back of my neck. "I just know that I'm not."

"You can't know that," I whispered.

"I do, Piper." He pulled away.

"No." I gripped his leather cut, pulling him against me. "You can't know that at all." Before he could protest again, I kissed him.

His stiff body relaxed under my touch. "You calm me," he said against my mouth.

"You drive me insane," I threw back at him.

He chuckled, placing a soft peck on my lips. "I don't know what it is about you, Piper."

"I can say the same for you," I told him, brushing my fingers through his dark hair. "How are you getting home?" I would have to move my car later on once the other cars filed out from the party.

"Don't worry about me." He kissed my forehead. "I have someone who will pick me up."

"Are you going to come to the party?" *Please say yes.*

"I shouldn't but that's never stopped me before." Jaron winked.

I smiled softly, pulling away from him.

His dark gray eyes met mine. They were warm and inviting, contradicting everything that made up Jaron Mercer.

Everything in me screamed for him to continue driving. To have him spend the night with me or take me away from there, but he was right. I wasn't sure anymore if I was ready for a relationship. We were both young. Still finding ourselves and all that shit. So I did the only thing I knew how. I left the vehicle and walked away.

### (Jaron)

Piper asked too many questions that I didn't know how to answer. At first, I wasn't ready for a relationship. But now, I wasn't so sure. Although she had been the only woman I ever fucked more than once, other men were involved. Men who were supposed to be my friends. But it wasn't their fault. It was mine.

A car drove past me, slowed down, and reversed. The passenger side window rolled down, revealing the very twins I was thinking about.

"Hey," I muttered, sticking my hands in my jeans pockets.

"Hey." Ashton nodded his head. "You're not coming to Gigi's party?"

"Not sure yet." I had to make a few calls and clear my head, so I started walking away from Piper's house. Brody being there wouldn't stop me from showing up.

"I'm sure Piper would want you to join us," Ashton said.

Aiden smacked him.

"What are you getting at?" I bit out, taking a step toward them.

"Nothing really." Ashton shrugged. "But we do know that you've been sleeping with our girl."

"Fuck," Aiden growled, parking the car. He got out of the vehicle and came around to the passenger side. "Ignore my brother. He's an ass. And she's not our girl," he corrected Ashton.

Ashton grunted. "Whatever."

"What do you want?" I crossed my arms under my chest, ignoring their banter. "I feel like your brother is wanting to start a fight. Although there's two of you, you both know I could kick your asses with my hands tied behind my back." I proved it once. Ashton ended up with a broken nose and Aiden's shoulder had been dislocated. That was over who was the strongest. But this was over a woman. A broken nose and a dislocated shoulder would be the least of their problems.

"We don't want to start any shit," Aiden told me, leaning against the side of his black muscle car. The beast was a beauty, and it reminded me of my Aunt Zillah's car.

"Then what do you want?" I checked my wrist. "I'm late."

"For what? You're not even wearing a watch, fucker," Ashton threw at me.

"Come out here and say that shit to my face if you have a problem, asshole." I was sick of this. We were friends after having grown up together. Even though I lived a few hours away, my parents brought me to this town every summer for as long as I could remember. But right now, Ashton was starting to piss me off.

"No." Aiden pushed off the side of the car. "Listen. Whatever is going on between you and Piper, it needs to end. She deserves better."

"What?" I laughed. "Like both of *you*?"

Aiden's jaw clenched. "We just want her happy and we want what's best for her."

"Right." I scoffed. "Both of you are only worried about competition."

"Jaron," Aiden said gently.

"I am not having this conversation with you." I didn't kiss and tell. Paris was Piper's and my little secret. Everything we did was between us only. Even though I kept pushing her away, I was man enough to admit that I had feelings for her. Hell, who wouldn't? And clearly, I was standing across from two men who felt the same way.

"Fuck it, let's just get out of here and go to the party," Ashton said.

"So are we going to throw away years of friendship over some chick?" Aiden asked.

"Aiden, we all know that Piper isn't just some *chick*." And with that, I walked away. They loved her. Or Aiden sure as hell did. I hadn't want to ruin our friendship, but I couldn't control myself around Piper either. I needed her like I needed my next breath, but I was too much of a pussy to admit that. I wasn't ready to settle down. Was I?

*Fuck.*

# SIX

*Piper*

**HEADING INTO THE** party, I realized then that I forgot the bags of ice. They were probably melted by now anyway.

"Hey, Piper." Gigi stopped when she saw my empty hands. "Where's the ice?"

"I … uh …"

She waved a hand in front of her. "No worries. We have lots. I just wanted some extra in case we ran out." She pulled me in for a quick hug. "You okay?"

I squeezed her. "I am." I needed a drink.

"Good. There's a bottle of wine for you in the fridge. It's your favorite."

"You're the best."

She fluffed her dark hair. "I know."

I laughed.

Grabbing the bottle of wine from the fridge, I poured myself a glass and brought the bottle with me out into the backyard. My name was called. I waved. Most of these people I had gone to school with. Being in a small town, we all grew up together, but I would never consider them friends. The only people I had been close to, were the ones I was raised with.

Finding a large group of people standing outside, I made my way to the patio set. Sitting on one of the couches, the hairs on the back of my neck stood on end. I looked around me just as the twins came closer.

Ashton and Aiden sat on either side of me.

"How's it going, Piper?" Ashton asked, placing his arm on the back of the couch behind me.

"Fine." I was too tired to tell them to leave me alone. Thankfully, they didn't hint for more or take it further.

"We ran into Jaron," Aiden told me, placing his ankle on his opposite knee.

"Oh?" My heart jumped. "What did he want?"

"Oh, you know. The usual." Ashton shrugged. "To chitchat."

I scoffed. "Jaron doesn't chitchat. What did you guys talk about?"

"You, Piper." Ashton ran his finger up the side of my neck, sending a shiver down my spine.

I took a large gulp from my glass of wine and stood from the couch. "I don't know what you guys want but you need to stop this."

"You know what we want." Ashton looked at his brother before meeting my gaze. "You. Just you."

"What we did was a mistake," I murmured, slumping onto a chair, putting some distance between me and the twins. "I never meant to lead you on." Guilt weighed heavily on my shoulders. I didn't want to hurt anyone. At all. I just wanted Jaron. That was it. Even before Paris, I knew something was off with what I was doing with Ashton and Aiden. My heart had never been in it. It was fun. But that was it.

"It was a mistake that we kept doing over and over again," Ashton reminded me.

My cheeks burned. I glanced down at the cup in my hand, running my finger over the rim. It was fun with the twins. We agreed in the beginning that it was just sex but now they wanted more. I had nothing against people who wanted to be in relationships with more than one person, and maybe it would have been my thing if Jaron wasn't in the picture. But since he was, I wanted to be just friends with the twins. But I knew that would never happen. They were safe, where Jaron wasn't. But *he* was who I wanted. I was addicted to the unknown. He was exciting and dangerous. It was what I needed.

*"I can't wait for the day I get to play with that little masochist inside of you."*

My body heated at the mere idea of what Jaron suggested. I wasn't sure how we would explore that side of me, but I hoped that he was right. I wanted to play. I wanted to explore. And I wanted to embrace the dark side of sex.

"You're thinking about him."

My eyes popped to Ashton's. "Did I ever tell you I wanted a relationship?"

He frowned.

"Did I ever hint for more? No. We got drunk. I had a shitty day at work after getting groped by dirty old men and you two made me feel better. I can't deal with this right now." I grabbed the bottle of wine and poured myself another glass. "Can we please talk about something else?"

"Fine." Aiden passed a glance at Ashton. "How's Jaron?"

I huffed, my cheeks burning.

Ashton chuckled.

"You guys are assholes," I mumbled, rising from the couch. As soon as I turned, I bumped right into … My eyes widened. "Jaron."

"Hello, Piper." His steel-gray eyes flicked over my head. "Problem?"

"Who invited you?"

I glared at Ashton over my shoulder. "Don't be rude. He's friends with all of us."

"Some more than others," Ashton mumbled, taking a swig of his beer.

"If you have something to say," I snapped. "Say it."

"Nope. Nothing at all." Ashton glanced between us both. "Nothing to say at all."

"I need another drink." Aiden stood and walked past us. "Ashton."

Ashton jumped from the couch and stopped in front of us. "He better be worth it, Piper." And with that, he walked away.

"Am I worth it, Piper?"

I shivered at the deep voice rumbling through me. "I'm going to go find Gigi," I told Jaron when, really, I just used that as an excuse to get away from him. From *all* of them.

### (Jaron)

I wasn't going to attend the party. Especially when Brody would be there, if he wasn't there already. I hadn't seen him as of yet. But when Gigi called me, telling me to watch over Piper, I couldn't resist. I had a sense that she was rooting for Piper and me. There was a hurdle in the way of me being with Piper, but I wasn't sure what it was exactly. We worked well together and hell, the sex was so fucking good.

Was I ready to settle down? I wasn't sure, but what I did know was that I didn't want her seeing anyone else. Hell, I wasn't seeing anyone else either.

I stood off to the side, nursing a beer and watching Piper. She stood with Gigi and a couple of other guys I had recognized from previous parties Gigi had thrown. They were harmless, especially when they caught me looking every so often.

My phone vibrated, indicating an incoming text.

**Cyrus: You good?**

**Me: Yup.**

**Sammy: Where are you?**

**Me: Party.**

**Cyrus: We're less than five minutes away if anything goes down.**

**Me: Good.**

I put my phone away appreciating that I wasn't truly alone and that Piper was safe. Even if I wasn't around, she would always be safe.

Cyrus and Sammy were a few years older than me and had been the brothers I never had. We were family, whether we were blood related or not. That fact alone didn't matter. I would lay my life on the line for them and they would, in turn, do the same for me.

My phone vibrated again.

Glancing at the small screen, I saw that a text had come in from an unknown number. My eyes popped up, landing on Brody standing across the yard. The fucker nodded once.

The tiny hairs on the back of my neck rose. He bothered me in ways I had never come across before. I knew some vile men. His father being one of them. But Brody Davies was different. On the outside, he was nice and innocent, but get him alone or piss him off and he would snap. My uncle was right. He was way too clean. His record was perfect. No one's record was perfect. Even if they never got caught, they still did something. Anything. But Brody hadn't. At all.

A laugh sounded a few feet away. That same laugh made my dick leak and my mouth water.

Brody's eyes followed the sound, landing on Piper who stood with Gigi, Meadow, and a few other girls. Gigi said something, using her hands animatedly, causing bubbles of laughter to erupt from the group.

My phone vibrated again.

I glanced down.

**Unknown: You shouldn't be at the party.**

**Me: You should mind your own business.**

**Unknown: You're in my town. You _are_ my business.**

**Me: You're not being very discreet, Mayor.**

**Unknown: I have no idea what you're talking about.**

_Bastard._

# BEFORE US

## (Piper)

"Have you girls talked to Luna?" I asked Gigi and Meadow.

"No." Gigi pulled her hair back into a tight ponytail. "I think she has her hands full with Zach."

I nodded. Luna was another friend who had finally started dating her crush. Zach Porter was Jaron's cousin and another one who was silent and broody. It seemed that Luna had been the only one to ever put a smile on his face.

"How are things going with you and those bikers?" I asked Meadow, waggling my eyebrows.

Meadow laughed, taking a sip of her wine. "So good. I like that they don't make me feel like a little girl. Not that it would be an issue if they did. You know that whole Daddy Dom thing and all, but it's not really my scene."

"Daddy Dom?" Gigi repeated, frowning.

Meadow patted her hand. "You need to read more."

Gigi blushed. "I'm so naïve."

"Nah. You just know what you want and that's not one of them." I shrugged. "I wouldn't worry about it."

"I don't even know what I want." Gigi looked around her. Her gaze landed on something that caused the red in her cheeks to become even more pronounced. "I feel like a dirty old woman."

"You *are* a dirty old woman." Meadow laughed.

"Is there something wrong with me?" Gigi asked, her brows narrowing. "Guys my own age don't do it for me. Hell, Vincent's more mature than them."

I followed her gaze. Vincent Junior stood off with some of his friends. He was Luna's younger brother and while he was much younger than us, he was a good guy and was highly mature for his age. "He's only a few years younger than you. Luna is only a couple years younger than Zach."

"That's different," Gigi muttered.

"How? Sunny and Shade are twenty years older than me." Meadow patted her own shoulder. "I'm so proud of myself right now."

We laughed.

"Listen, Gigi. Vincent is young but he's mature." I had to admit that Gigi was right though. Vincent Junior *was* good-looking.

"True." Gigi sighed. "He probably hasn't noticed me anyway."

I bit back a scoff, but I understood her doubts. Hell, I had them about Jaron and myself. My body heated, and that was when I remembered that my thong was currently sitting in Jaron's pocket.

Gigi and I both stood at the same time, bumping our hands together and knocking over our wine.

Giggles erupted between us.

A red stain spread on my dress. I wanted to change anyway but at least this would give me a better excuse.

"I'm so sorry." Gigi pouted. "What a waste of wine."

"No problem." I patted her hand. "I was going to change anyway."

I excused myself. As much as I enjoyed feeling Jaron's cum on my thighs, it gave me a reason to have a moment alone. And also a moment to grab more wine. More wine was always needed.

Once I reached my room, I went in search of something new to wear.

A soft knock on the door a moment later, startled me.

"Coming," I called out, wiping the wet spot on my dress. Of course I had to wear white. Why would it make sense not to wear white when I was drinking red wine? I mentally smacked myself.

Opening the door, I stared up into Brody's deep green eyes. My stomach twisted as I remembered the new information I was given about him. Knowing I had to play it cool and not act like anything was wrong, I smiled up at him.

"Hey, Brody. I was just cleaning my dress. Or trying to." I looked down at the stain that was now pink. "Hopefully I can get this out. I actually like this dress." Even though it had only been a few dollars, it was comfy, and it was soft. I should have bought—I was suddenly shoved back a step.

Brody closed the door behind him, clicking the lock into place. His eyes roamed down the length of me, his tongue swiping along his bottom lip.

My heart started racing. Ice-cold fear gripped my spine. "Brody?" my voice cracked. "W-What's going on?"

He didn't meet my gaze. His lips moved like he was mumbling to himself, but no words came out.

"Hey," I said gently. "What's wrong?"

He took a step toward me, forcing me back.

"Brody." I held up my hands, trying so damn hard not to spook him. He had always been kind. Gentle. A little off but his father was the mayor, so he was constantly in the spotlight. We thought it had to do with that, but this situation proved differently. Him being nice was too good to be true. "I don't know what's wrong but—"

"Shut up," he whispered. "Shut up. Shut up. *Shut up.*" His voice rose, sending that ice-cold fear racing over me into undeniable amounts of terror.

"Please leave," I demanded softly. "I won't tell anyone." And I especially wouldn't tell Jaron.

"I saw you with him," Brody finally said. He rubbed his nape, his gaze flicking back and forth but still not meeting my eyes. "I saw you with them. The twins. *Him.*"

"With who?"

Brody reached his hand behind him. It came back a second later with a knife in it.

My world tilted on its axis. This was it. This was how I was going to die, or worse.

"I like you, Piper." Brody met my gaze that time. "I've always liked you, but you didn't like me back. I don't know why. I have money. I have a lot of money. I could make you fall in love with me. Whether you like it or not. You will be mine. I'll see to it. No matter who gets in the way, you will always be mine."

"We're friends," I told him, backing up until I hit the edge of my dresser. "We've always just been friends."

"Yeah." Brody chuckled, the sound cold and vile. "You see. That doesn't work for me. If I can't have you, no one's going to have you. I don't give a shit who they are. It kind of sucks that I have to do this here though. I like your friends. They have nothing to do with this. It's all you, Piper. You and that slutty little body of yours. You've been prancing around here half naked ever since you got back from Paris. Is that what you learned over there? How to be a whore?"

My blood burned at what he was accusing me of. "I'm not a whore, and I don't dress like it either."

"No? You don't? I've seen you with the twins. I like them though. But Jaron? Come on, Piper. You could do so much better than him. He's a biker." Brody took a step toward me.

"Please, Brody. We can talk about this." I reached behind me, trying to find something on my dresser that I could use as a weapon, but there was nothing. My dad had tried getting me to have a gun, but I refused. Even if I kept it in a locked case, we threw too many parties. I didn't want to take the chance that someone would stumble into my room and find it. I suddenly regretted that decision.

"Talk?" Brody laughed. "What are we going to talk about, Piper?"

Taking a breath, I ran around him and jumped onto my bed when my feet were pulled out from beneath me. I cried out, struggling against him. I kicked and fought with all of the strength I could muster. My foot landed against Brody's crotch, making him grunt, but it didn't stop him from ripping at my clothes. His fingers dug into my sides, his knee pushing into the small of my back.

I winced, attempting to push him off of me but he was too damn strong. "Brody, please stop this."

Brody removed his knee from my back and towered over me. With his fist in my hair, he leaned down to my ear. "You see, Piper. I do want to do this. Because no matter what, I can get away with it. I wonder what would happen if Jaron walked in. There would be a struggle, naturally. But people will think I actually fought him off. That I was the one to stop him from raping you."

My eyes widened. "W-What are you saying?"

"I'm the hero, baby. I'm *your* hero." With a firm grip on my head, he leaned back and slammed his fist into the side of my face.

Spots danced in my vision. Agony screamed through my cheek. My lip split, a metallic taste coating my tongue.

Brody turned me onto my back and knelt between my legs. "You're so fucking beautiful. Why couldn't you fall for a guy like me? Why him?" Wrapping a hand around my throat, he grazed the other up my thigh, pushing it beneath the hem of my dress.

Bile rose to my throat, when I remembered I had no panties on. He would see me. Just a little more and he would see every inch of me. A part that had belonged to Jaron since Paris. I struggled, trying to grab the fabric from him but he was too strong for me. "Please, Brody. Stop this."

Squeezing my throat, he towered over me. "I want you to look into my eyes when I fuck your soul."

I whimpered. "Please stop."

"That's right." He licked up the side of my face. "Beg for it. Isn't that what you do for Jaron? I bet he has you crawling on the ground for him like a little bitch in heat. You're a fucking slut. Sleeping with the twins. Now Jaron. And then me."

My stomach twisted. "No." I grabbed his hand around my throat, digging my nails into his skin, but that only seemed to make him squeeze harder. The lack of air burned through my lungs. I gasped for breath, spots dancing in my vision. "Brody," I croaked. "Stop."

A heavy fist slammed into the side of my head and then my stomach. It forced the fight from me. No matter what I did, I couldn't push him off. I couldn't scream. I couldn't fight. I couldn't overpower him. I had no idea that Brody was this strong. He was smaller than Jaron. Much smaller.

"Brody," I whispered.

He leaned down to my ear. "I will make it so you never forget me."

He was right. I wouldn't. I never would.

### (Jaron)

"Hey, Jaron." Gigi came toward me, followed by Meadow.

"Hey." I nodded. "What's up?"

"Have you seen Piper?" Gigi looked behind her over her shoulder. "We bumped into each other and spilled our wine. Some landed on her dress and she was going to change."

"That was half an hour ago," Meadow added.

I glanced around the backyard, not seeing Brody anywhere in sight. "Shit."

"Jaron?" Gigi raised an eyebrow.

I pulled my phone out of my pocket and texted Sammy and Cyrus.

**Me: Get over here. *Now.***

If he hurt her, I would kill him. I would make him beg for his life. I would rip off every part of him that touched her.

Storming into the house, I slowed my steps to a walk, not wanting to cause a scene.

"Jaron?" Gigi followed me. "What's going on?"

"Which room is Piper's?" I demanded, inching my way down the hall.

"Last one on the left." Her eyes were wide. "I can't find Brody."

My stomach clenched. "Stay out here," I told her as Sammy and Cyrus appeared around the corner.

Gigi jumped. "Who are you?"

"They're with me," I told her.

She nodded. "Okay."

Sammy and Cyrus came toward me.

I held up my hand, signaling for them to follow me. Once we neared the end of the hallway, I stood outside Piper's door. I heard muffled voices but couldn't make out anything that was being said. Trying the door, I realized then that it was locked. Sammy gently pushed me out of the way and picked it with the tools he had kept in his pocket at all times. Thank fuck for that.

The door unlocked.

"Stay out here," I told them. I wasn't sure what I would be walking in on, but I didn't want them to see anything they shouldn't see. Especially if it belonged to Piper.

Slowly opening the door, my vision became clouded when my eyes landed on what laid before me. Brody was on top of Piper. Her dress was torn. Her face was badly beaten. His fist was in her hair. Her dress was pushed up and over her ass, but he was still clothed. The flesh of her rear was red like he had spanked her over and over.

I didn't know if he had finished the act or not. It didn't matter. The fact that he started it in the first place, earned him death.

Blood pounded in my ears and before I knew what I was doing, I charged for him.

Both of us fell to the ground beside the bed. My fists hit his face repeatedly. He struggled beneath me, but I was too strong for him. I should stop. I knew I should have stopped, but the rage inside of me controlled my actions.

I vaguely heard my name being called. Over and over again.

*Jaron. Jaron. Jaron.*

But I couldn't stop. I couldn't quit. He had to hurt. He had to die. Brody was a slimy fucker, but we could never prove anything thanks to who his father was, but this time we had proof. We had something.

"Jaron."

A metallic taste coated my tongue. Blood splattered my face and clothes. The skin on my knuckles split with each hit against the bones in Brody's face.

"Jaron." Warm, gentle arms wrapped around my shoulders, pulling me off of him. I could have fought but I didn't.

Brody stared up at me. His eyes and face now swollen and bloody.

# BEFORE US

It wasn't enough.
But it had to do.

# SEVEN

## *Piper*

**YOU SEE IT** on the news. Hear about it in passing while at school. Maybe a friend of a friend experienced it. But you would never think that it could happen to you. You're safe. You're smart. You don't go out at night. You don't walk down an alleyway alone. You keep with friends. You have a buddy system. You think you're good and in the clear until one day it's your friend who tries to rape you.

My heart raced. My blood pounded in my ears. My hands shook.

Jaron pushed away from me and rose to his full height. He pulled a gun from the back of his pants and shot him.

My heart jumped. Although the sound had been quieter than I expected, knowing he had a silencer on the pistol, the shot still rang in my ears.

I squeezed my eyes shut, shaking my head. This couldn't be happening. I was dreaming. It was a fucked up nightmare. A shiver trembled through me. I needed clothes. I needed to get changed.

"Piper."

"I-I need to get changed." I sat up, pulling at my tattered dress. Clothes that were ripped and shredded. Clothes that hung off of me. Was I dressed too slutty? Did I lead Brody on? Was I a tease?

"Piper."

My wide eyes stared at the man who saved me.

Jaron's gaze met mine.

"Is he ..." My stomach churned. I had never seen a dead body before. Only in movies but this was nothing like them. This was real life. This was ... this was worse.

Jaron didn't move. He only stared at me. Was he waiting for me to freak out? To leave and tell everyone what happened?

I slowly pushed myself from the bed. Jaron stepped over Brody's lifeless form and crashed into me. Cupping my face, he forced me to look up at him.

"Say it," he demanded, turning me away from Brody. "Say it, Piper."

"I ... I don't know what you want me to say." I shivered, my heart racing hard behind the walls of my rib cage.

"What did you see?" He shielded me from Brody. "Tell me."

"Brody." I swallowed hard. "Brody's dead."

"Yes." Jaron wrapped his arms around me. "Do you still want me?"

"You saved me," I said, ignoring his question.

"I would go to hell for you, Piper." He kissed my cheek. "Remember that."

I looked away. Neither of us were ready for a confession like that but yet, he said it anyway.

"Tell me what you want me to do," Jaron said, pushing me back into the corner.

"What do you mean?" My heart was thundering in my ears, an impending headache threatening to explode through my mind at the same time.

"We can do this the legal way and call the cops, or I can have my boys clean this up. No questions asked." Jaron pinched my chin, forcing me to look up at him. "We will do whatever you want. But Brody was the mayor's son. This won't go away."

"So we have to call the cops." I wasn't sure how his boys could make Brody disappear.

"Just say the word, Piper."

"I ... I don't know. I feel ..." I shivered. I should have felt guiltier. Shouldn't I have? Brody was going to ... "He was going to rape me." I gripped Jaron's leather jacket, leaning my head against his chest. "But he didn't. God ... I ..."

"Yeah, Piper." Jaron cupped my nape, brushing his thumb back and forth over the spot just beneath my ear. "He was." He gently pulled my head back, running his fingers over the bruises on my face. "I've seen a lot of shit. I've been through a lot too but seeing that ... seeing him ..." His jaw clenched.

"I can't ... I don't ..." My breathing became labored, tears burned my eyes.

"Look at me." Jaron gently tugged my head back. "What he did, is *not* your fault. What he said to you, none of that was true. You hear me?"

I nodded, the tears falling freely down my cheeks. "I've never seen that side of him. He's always been nice to us. I actually thought he was gay at one point. I thought maybe his fiancée leaving him turned him or something. I thought..."

"Bastards like that will never let you know that they're a rapist." Jaron leaned down to meet my gaze. "You hear me?"

I nodded again. "I need out of here."

"Tell me what you want to do."

I glanced back at Brody's body. "We should call the cops."

"And tell them what?"

"You're asking me?"

"I am." Jaron brushed a finger down my jaw. "This is all you, Piper. Your choice. Whatever you want."

"I … I don't know what I want. I want this night to be over. I want us to be happy. I want to forget. I just … I want you." I gripped his jacket, leaning my forehead against his chest.

"I don't deserve you, Piper." Jaron cupped my nape. "You can come in now."

I glanced up, finding him on his cell.

He caught my gaze, his gray eyes darkening even more. He ended the call, putting his phone back in his pocket. About a minute later, there was a knock on the door.

I jumped. "Jaron."

"Trust me." He kissed the top of my head and released me. Walking toward the door to my bedroom, he opened it.

A large man filled the doorway. He glanced my way, nodded once and stepped into my room. He was followed by another man who looked identical to him but smaller.

"Piper, that large fucker is Cyrus, and this is his brother, Sammy," Jaron said, closing the door and clicking the lock into place. "Guys, this is Piper."

"We finally meet." Sammy came toward me and stuck out his hand. "I wish it could be under different circumstances."

"Me too." I returned the handshake. "Twins?"

"Yeah, kiddo." He nodded toward Cyrus. "Although this fucker beefed up on me so now I look like a damn pussy next to him."

Cyrus only grunted. "What do you want us to do?"

"Piper?"

I turned to Jaron. "What?"

"Tell him," he said gently.

I glanced at Cyrus who now stood over Brody's body. "I ... I feel like we should call the cops but ..."

"Nothing will happen to you, Piper." Jaron moved to my side, hooking an arm around my shoulders. "I promise you that. I'll go to jail first."

"No." I shoved out of his grip. "You could be there for years. If I say it was self-defense."

"No," all three men barked at once.

"But—"

"I said no." Jaron took my hands, bringing them up to his mouth and placed soft pecks on my knuckles. "Call the cops." He glanced over his shoulder. "I came in, found him trying to rape Piper and pulled him off. He swung at me and ended up pulling a gun on me. Isn't that right?" He looked at me then. "Even if you pulled the trigger yourself, you could have it worse."

"How is that even fair?" I gaped at him.

"It's not." Jaron kissed my fingertips. "He pulled a gun on me. Right, Piper?"

I swallowed hard.

Jaron handed Cyrus his gun. Cyrus wiped it off with a black cloth and placed the gun in Brody's hand.

"The mayor has it out for us," Cyrus said. "Has since our dads were kids. This won't end well, Jaron."

"I know." Jaron cupped my face. "Like I said, Piper. I would go to hell for you."

"Why?" I whispered, covering his hand.

"I think you know why." Something flashed behind his eyes. Although he had never said the words, I knew what he meant. But it wasn't time. It could possibly never be the right time. But I still wanted to hear them.

"Tell me," I demanded. "Please."

"No, baby." He swallowed noisily. "I don't want to say them and be taken from you. When I say them, when I say those fucking words, Piper, it'll be when you're wrapped around me."

Tears threatened to burn my eyes.

"He tried shooting Jaron but before that happened, Jaron was able to take him out. Isn't that right, Piper?" Cyrus asked me.

A breath left me at the lie they expected me to tell. Could I do it? Could I do it for him?

"Yes," I finally said. "That's right."

"Good girl." Jaron kissed my forehead. "I could go away for a while," he whispered.

"Even if I testify?" I leaned back, staring up at him.

"I don't think that would matter. The mayor has it out for bikers in general. He always has for our family and crew. He'll probably throw me behind bars just out of spite. Especially now that it involves his son." Jaron brushed his thumb along the length of my jaw. "But you'll be safe. No matter what happens." He looked over his shoulder. "Sammy and Cyrus will make sure you're good."

"That's not their job." I pushed out of his hold.

"Piper."

I spun on Jaron. "What? I can't do this without you. I know we went into this because it was fun, but I need more from you." I didn't care that we weren't alone, he needed to hear what I had to say. "I like you, Jaron. I like you a lot. Paris was the best night of my life. And then you came here and …" My chest tightened. "I need more."

Jaron closed the distance between us, wrapping his big body around mine and hugged me to him. "I don't deserve more from you."

My eyes burned. Running my hands inside his leather cut, I pushed my face against his chest and inhaled. He smelled of sweat and spice. Everything that made up him. The man I couldn't stop thinking about. The man I needed but pushed away at the same time.

"What about ... what about us?" I had gone into this wanting nothing more than a good time, but it wasn't true. As much as I wanted it to be. It was never true.

"Don't wait for me, Piper." He kissed my head.

"Don't." I pushed him. "Will you give us a moment?" I asked Cyrus and Sammy. "Please."

They glanced at Jaron who nodded, but instead of leaving, Jaron tugged me into the bathroom. Shutting the door behind him, he leaned against it and waited.

"You can't tell me to not wait for you," I finally said. "No matter how long you're in jail for—"

"Piper," he growled, coming toward me. "You deserve more than that."

"I don't care," I sobbed, tears streaming down my face. "I need you."

"Fuck." Jaron crashed into me, wrapping himself around me. All we did was hold each other. I wasn't sure how long we stood like that. After what felt like an eternity, he pulled back. "I got blood on you."

I swallowed hard, looking down at myself. "I'm sure they'll want this for evidence."

"When I saw him on top of you. His marks on you." Jaron pinched my chin, forcing me to look up at him. "I'll never forgive myself for letting you walk away from me tonight."

"Don't do that." My voice cracked. "It's not your fault."

He cupped my cheek, brushing his hand to the back of my head and held me against him. "Yeah, I'd like to report an attempted rape and murder," he muttered.

A sob left me when I realized he had called the police.

"I just found you." I pulled him tighter against me. "And now you're leaving. You're leaving me."

"I'm sorry, Piper." He pulled back and leaned his forehead against mine. "I'm so fucking sorry. I never should have pushed you away. I should have spent more time with you in Paris instead of just fucking you."

"I'm the one who left you," I reminded him.

"But that was on me."

"I was scared." I stared up at him. "My feelings for you scare me."

"I know, baby." He placed a hard peck on my mouth. "I know."

Tears rolled freely down my cheeks. This was it. He would be taken from me for who knew how long. But no matter what he said, I would wait for him. Paris didn't happen for no reason. We were meant to be. I knew we had a lot of shit to work through, but he was mine and I was his. Before we even began, there was something there. Paris reiterated that fact.

"Piper." As soon as my name left Jaron's lips, a hard knock sounded on the door. It was shoved open suddenly, revealing two police officers.

"No." I gripped Jaron's jacket. "Jaron, please."

"I'll go quietly with you," he told the officers, ignoring me. "As long as you don't cuff me."

They glanced between each other.

"Fine," the one officer said. "Don't make me regret being nice."

Jaron kissed my forehead. "I have to go."

"Please. I lo—"

"What did I say?" he snapped.

My chest tightened.

One of the officers pulled him from me.

The last thing I saw when they took him out of the bathroom was the look of pain in Jaron's dark-gray eyes.

I fell to my knees, sobs crashing through me. I couldn't do this. I wasn't strong enough. My heart felt like it was being ripped into a million tiny pieces. Jaron was an asshole most times, but he was mine. He had always been mine and, before we could move forward, we were set completely back.

# EPILOGUE

## JARON

**I RAN MY** thumb over the black and white photo in my hand. It had been the only thing keeping me going. I pushed Piper away and yet she was still able to get to me. She wasn't giving up on us. I didn't deserve her. I didn't deserve any of this, but I craved her just the same. I wanted her happy. I waited for the day I could put a smile on her face and make her laugh. I waited for the day I could tell her how I felt and hear her say the same.

*"This is just sex, Piper," I said, kissing the corner of her mouth as I ripped her panties free from her body. "That's all I want."*

*"Good." She pushed me back. "Because that's all you're going to get."*

It had felt like years since our night together in Paris. I didn't know she was there until I saw her sitting at the little café that would change both of our worlds forever.

I stood, stuffing the picture into my pocket and headed to the phones. Thankfully I had been a good boy and still had phone privileges. I was still awaiting trial but needed to keep my nose clean. I didn't want to be holed up in this hell any longer than necessary.

Picking up the receiver, I dialed the number that had been engrained in my mind from the moment Piper gave it to me.

"Jaron." Piper's sweet voice washed over me, giving me the strength I needed to move forward.

"Yeah, sweet girl. It's me."

"God, I've missed your voice."

"I'm sorry for pushing you away. I'm sorry for everything."

"Don't. You can try pushing me away all you want but I'm here. I'm not going anywhere, Jaron. And I know when you get out, we'll have a lot of shit to work through but …"

"I got the picture." I rested my arm on top of the phone.

"I'm glad."

"I wish I could be there for you," I told her, my voice thick. "For both of you."

"I know but you will be. I'm waiting."

"Fuck, Piper. I like the sound of that."

She laughed lightly. "I'm ready, Jaron."

Although she said the words and I felt them down to the marrow of my bones, I wasn't sure how ready either of us were. Or if we ever would be.

# BONUS

## JARON

**"I'M PROUD OF** you, son." My dad smiled at me from the other side of the glass.

My heart swelled.

The question was on the tip of my tongue, but I didn't want to ask. It hurt. Fuck me it hurt. Not being able to hold Piper. Not seeing her. Not talking to her. But she had to move on. She deserved better. I knew she wouldn't listen to me though. A part of me was proud of that fact. I couldn't wait for the day I could leave this place and have her back in my arms. But I also wasn't stupid. I would have to earn the right to touch her again. To earn her heart. To earn her damn love. I should have told her how I felt.

"Piper's doing well." My dad grunted. "Well, as good as can be expected."

I nodded, gripping the phone receiver tightly in my hand. It had been a few months since I had seen her. Since I talked to her. Weeks since I was locked away in this shit hole.

"You need to keep your nose clean, son," my dad told me. "Trust me. Please fucking trust me. I need you smart and to use your head."

I frowned. "Why wouldn't I?"

His jaw clenched. Although his graying beard had grown in some, I could still see the typical clench of his jaw he always did when he was hesitating over what to say next.

"What's going on?" I sat forward when my father didn't respond. "Is it Piper? Is she okay?"

"You need to see her."

It was on the tip of my tongue to refuse but I knew I couldn't. Tomorrow was the trial I had been waiting for. That we all had been waiting for.

"What's going on?" I asked instead.

"Just trust me." My dad leaned forward, searching my face. "You already know. Don't you?"

"I have no idea what you're talking about." The black and white picture sat in my pocket. I found out at Cyrus and Sammy's last visit that she had them mail it to me. My girl was good. Even though I had pushed her away in the beginning, she was stubborn and fighting.

*Keep fighting, baby. I'm here.*

"Jaron."

"Listen, Cyrus and Sammy are watching over her. I'll see her tomorrow at the trial. She'll vouch for me. I know she will."

"I know she will too." My dad gave me a soft smile. "I have no doubt about that."

"I should go." I needed to call her.

"Keep your head up, Jaron," my dad warned. "And trust no one within these walls."

"I know. Give Mom a hug for me."

*Wait for me, Piper. Don't listen to me. Please don't listen to me. I need you. I'm coming for you, sweet girl.*

And when I saw her again, I was never letting her go.

# BEFORE US

## (Piper)

Jaron had been charged with involuntary manslaughter. Even though we both knew that it was definitely voluntary.

Being called up to the stand to testify, had been one of the hardest things I had ever done. The mayor had been there and that didn't make me feel any better. He was slimy, his eyes raking over my body. Bile rose to my throat, just thinking about it.

That had been a few months ago and now I was spending most of my time, waiting for the phone call that Jaron was being released.

As if on cue, my phone rang, startling me. My heart thumped. There was no way.

"Hello?" I greeted whoever was on the other end.

"Piper."

My eyes widened. "Jaron."

"I'm ready, baby," he told me.

"Are you getting out? Please tell me that you're getting out," I pleaded. I needed him. We had so much to work through, but I couldn't do it without him at my side.

"I am, Piper." Jaron sighed. "Tomorrow."

"I'll be there," I told him. "I promise."

"Good." He paused. "Both of you?"

I smiled, bringing my knees up to my chest. "Yeah. Both of us."

"Thank fucking God."

"Jaron?" I said, picking at a fuzz on the blanket wrapped around me.

"Yeah, baby?"

"Do you think we can do this?" I needed him to voice his thoughts. I needed to know that I wasn't crazy for thinking there was something between us. That we could make this work.

"If I have you, if I have both of you, Piper. Yes, I think we can do this. Will it be easy? No. No relationship is. But I know how I feel about you."

I dropped my knees, sitting Indian-style, and sat forward. "Tell me."

"Not yet. I can't."

"Not until I'm wrapped around you." I slumped back against the couch.

"Yeah, Piper. I need to look into your eyes when I say it. When you say it."

My chest tightened, a lump forming in my throat. "What time should I be there tomorrow?"

He gave me a time and our discussion quickly ended after that when he was told his time was up.

When the call was disconnected, I walked down the hall of my small house. I had just moved into it not too long ago. Boxes still needed to be unpacked but I wasn't worried about them at that point.

Once I reached a room at the end of the hall, I took a deep breath and entered. My thoughts traveled back to that night at the bar. Because of that night, a new life was created. Even though Jaron and I had things to work through, we had this. Together, we could conquer whatever was thrown in our path.

My heart beat hard for a man currently sitting behind bars. A man who saved me from a monster. A man I loved.

"I love you, Jaron," I whispered, finally voicing the words out loud. After all this time, I gave in to the feelings I had for him. Now I just needed tomorrow to come so we could take this to the next level. Even if it was just one step at a time, it was a step that I wanted to take.

With him.

### ***THE END***

Add Being Us (Next Generation, #4) to your TBR list:

### Goodreads -
https://www.goodreads.com/book/show/51377055-being-us

# ACKNOWLEDGEMENTS

First off, thank you to my team:
*Angie, Jennifer, Christina and Joanne.*
I couldn't do this without you. Because of you, I've become a better writer. I can't thank you enough for your patience and helping me perfect my stories.

My readers: Because of **you**, this story was created. I'm SO excited to bring you **The Next Generation**. Even though this trilogy isn't part of the series but a spin-off instead, I think you'll love it nonetheless. Jaron and Piper have been through so much and their story is too big to fit into one book. Or so Jaron tells me anyway.

But it's going to be fun, intense and such a crazy ride, I can't wait to give the kids their HEA's that they all deserve.

Authors and bloggers: Your support is everything. Thank you for taking a chance on me.

2020 is going to be filled with so many books!

J.M.

XX

# ABOUT

J.M. Walker is an Amazon bestselling author who also hit USA Today with Wanted: An Outlaw Anthology. She loves all things books, pigs and lip gloss. She is happily married to the man who inspires all of her Heroes and continues to make her weak in the knees every single day.

*"Above all, be the HEROINE of your own life..."* ~ Nora Ephron

**Website:** http://www.aboutjmwalker.com/
**Facebook:** https://www.facebook.com/jm.walker.author
**Reader Group:** https://www.facebook.com/groups/JMsJems/
**Twitter:** https://twitter.com/jmwlkr
**Instagram:** https://www.instagram.com/jmwlkr/
**Goodreads:** https://www.goodreads.com/author/show/5132169.J_M_Walker
**BookBub:** https://www.bookbub.com/authors/j-m-walker
**Amazon:** https://tinyurl.com/y7dpjkud
**Newsletter:** https://tinyurl.com/ya9hycak

**Want more? Head on over to my website for my complete backlist!**
https://www.aboutjmwalker.com/books